Gudrun Rogge-Wiest

Team Spirit

The Present

For all those who were part

of the network back then

All characters appearing in this work are fictitious.
Any resemblance to real persons, living or dead,
is purely coincidental.

Bibliografische Information der Deutschen Nationalbibliothek:
Die Deutsche Nationalbibliothek verzeichnet diese Publikation
in der Deutschen Nationalbibliografie; detaillierte bibliografische Daten sind im Internet über dnb.dnb.de abrufbar.

© 2023 Gudrun Rogge-Wiest
Verlag: BoD • Books on Demand GmbH, In de Tarpen 42,
22848 Norderstedt
Druck: Libri Plureos GmbH, Friedensallee 273, 22763
Hamburg

ISBN: 978-3-7597-7946-5

What it is

It is nonsense
says Reason.
It is what it is
says Love

It is bad luck
says Calculation.
It is nothing but pain
says Anxiety.

It is hopeless
says Understanding
It is what it is
says Love.

It is ridiculous
says Pride.
It is careless
says Prudence.

It is impossible
says Experience.
It is what it is
says Love.

Erich Fried (1921 – 1988)
Translation: Rogge-Wiest

Table of Contents

Chapter IV   **73**

Chapter V   **93**

Chapter 1

September 1999

The dessert

Teresa Rinaldi is in the kitchen of her shared flat. She whips together egg yolk and powdered sugar for a Tiramisu. She hopes that no-one will join her, now, because she is nervous. She wants the Tiramisu to be perfect, and as always when she wants to be perfect, she is scared that something will go wrong. What if she spoils the cream, for example? This would be a disaster, because tomorrow evening they are going to celebrate the extension of their collaborative research project. Their supervisor, Professor Dr Feldmann, has invited those colleagues from the other departments, who are also involved. Each of his staff members contributes some dessert. She offered to bring a Tiramisu.

Cautiously, she stirs in the mascarpone, then folds in the whipped egg whites gently. The cream does look good! Now it's time to pile up the Tiramisu in the big rectangular dish. She lays out the espresso-soaked ladyfingers, spreads cream on them, then overlays it with more ladyfingers and covers them with another blanket of cream. Finally, she sprinkles cocoa powder on it until there is no white shining through any more.

After a last critical look at her work she puts the dish onto the topmost shelf of the fridge, which she cleared beforehand. In order to remind her flat mates that she needs the dessert whole the next day she sticks a *Post It* note on the dish. Then she heads for her room.

She crosses over to the window in the half-light. The flat is on the fourth floor of a historical turn of the century town house, high enough to be able to see the sky above the houses opposite. At present it is glowing in various shades of red, the last rays of the setting sun. She stands gazing raptly for a little longer before she turns away to switch on the light.

Her room looks spacious not least because of its high ceiling, but perhaps also because it is sparsely furnished: a wardrobe, a desk with a chair, and on the wall opposite a book shelf and a bed. When she moved in Teresa had been glad that it was partially furnished because she had hardly any savings. The bed and the wardrobe made of gleaming reddish-brown wood belong to a past era, the late 19th or early 20th century. It set off the lighter wood and more sober design of her big desk and her book shelf, which she bought at the local branch of a big Swedish furniture chain. In order to keep out the orange gleam of the city night sky, which never goes completely dark, she hung up burgundy curtains made of an opaque fabric.

Turning away from the light switch, she faces her image in the mirror. She is slim and well-proportioned. Her features are finely chiselled but clear-cut. While gazing at herself searchingly, her forehead has wrinkled, and frown lines have appeared between her eyebrows. Alastair says that with her glasses on and her hair in a ponytail she looks like the very strict maths teacher he used to have. Amused by the thought of this she removes the hair tie and her glasses. As always, she is surprised at the difference. Only now do her almond-shaped green and brown eyes show to advantage against the background of her pale skin and the dark brown of her shoulder length wavy hair. She should let it down more often. Still, it gets on her nerves when wisps of it fall into her face while she is working. But she could wear contact lenses. So far she has shied away from the extra effort and expense

Since Sabrina joined their research team, she has become more conscious of her outward appearance. Of course, she is no match for a woman of such strong presence who puts herself in the limelight, as if this was the most natural thing in the world.

Is it possible to learn to be more outgoing? She doubts it. You'd probably have to start at a very young age. And would she still be herself, then?

She lifts her chin, which gives her a look of determination. This makes her laugh out loud. To work, she commands herself. She walks to her desk, switches the desk lamp on and takes the script for tomorrow's undergraduate seminar out of her bag in order to think her lesson plan through once more.

Anxiety

Immersed in the warm shallows of the sea, she is rocked gently back and forth, when, suddenly, a wave seizes her and her body hits the wet sand. Shortly after, another big wave washes over her and flings her further up the beach where she remains lying while the sea is sucked back with a protracted hissing sound in order to turn round and launch a new attack. While she is lying there covered by a multitude of drops of water, a cool breeze strokes her skin. She shivers, and when she opens her eyes, she is surprised that she is lying in her bed. Her legs and lower body are uncovered because part of her blanket has dropped over the edge. Teresa leans forward, picks it up and throws it over her legs. Now, she already feels much better. But it was not just the cold. Deep down, a sense of anxiety has remained. What might be its cause? She woke up from a dream in which she was floating in the sea and was flung on a beach by the surge. She was shaken by the impact, but her unease originated from a dream she had had earlier, a dream featuring Alastair. He kissed her farewell and then, walking away turned around waving once more, while at a distance on the opposite side of the road Sabrina appeared. She laughed showing two rows of perfect white teeth. Little golden ear-bands flashed among her blond curls, which, illuminated by the evening sun, shone in an orange tone and bobbed around her oval face like a lion´s mane. Under her hip-length unbuttoned black jacket she is wearing a form-fitting white top. Between it and her black trousers a narrow gap opens and closes in sync with her gait revealing a band of bronzed skin with a gemstone glittering in her navel.

Alastair and Sabrina, she thinks, while her heart contracts painfully. But it was just a dream. A nightmare. Anyway. Since Sabrina got one of the vacant positions as a doctoral candidate, the atmosphere has changed, for as the woman she is, she appeals to her colleagues as males. Now, you can hear the sound of banter and occasional loud laughter indicating Sabrina´s presence in the staff kitchen, even from a distance.

When they met in the kitchen or had lunch together before her time, Teresa felt comfortable because she was respected as a person. In other words, it didn´t matter so much that she was a woman. They talked about all kinds of things. When they discussed their work, she was in her element, but she also found it interesting, when they shared their thoughts about social and political topics or simply reported what they had done in their free time. The rapid back and forth of equivocal remarks in Sabrina´s presence, however, leaves her out of her depth. She is unsure when her colleagues cross the boundary to a flirt, and this fills her with a nagging inner unrest.

She has been together with Alastair for more than a year, now. Meanwhile, she stays over at his beautiful one-bedroom flat at the weekends and sometimes during the week, too. Only when she needs to be on her own does she retreat to her room in the shared flat.

Everyone on the team knows that they are a couple, although it is not immediately apparent. She prefers to keep a low profile at work. For her their love is a private matter, a bond between their souls, such as in these lines by John Donne, which Alastair printed out for her on a special card:

> *Our two souls therefore, which are one,*
> *though I must go, endure not yet*
> *a breach, but an expansion,*
> *like gold to airy thinness beat.*

How beautiful! With Sabrina on the scene, however, she is not so sure, anymore.

She can sometimes hardly hold herself back from enquiring, but she is aware that the spell of the words *I love you!* loses its power, when they are used too often. They agree on this. Besides, she takes care not to monopolize him, because he enjoys making new friends and getting a glimpse of their lives. It is as if he collected life stories. She, however, always struggles to overcome her reluctance, when someone new enters their familiar circle. But she gets along well with Fatima, the second doctoral candidate, with whom she shares her office, and with Mrs Lohr, Professor Feldmann´s secretary. When the women are by themselves, they often switch to more personal matters, which she likes.

She sighs. Feeling sad she permits herself to snuggle once more under her blanket, just for a few minutes, as she oughtn´t to arrive at the university too late. Because of the tiramisu she has to take the tram, which takes longer than riding there by bike. Resolutely, she sits up, pushes her blanket aside and swings her legs out of bed.

Coffee break

It is almost half past ten. Professor Dr Jakub Feldmann has locked his office door and is walking briefcase in hand along the corridor towards the staircase. From the office of his postdocs Rahul Sabharwal and Alastair Collins the sound of a lively conversation reaches his ear. A woman laughs out loud. Sabrina Kühnel. He stops by the open door looking in to say a few friendly words. Sabrina is seated on the long desk at the window between the two men, probably for lack of a third chair. She props herself up with her hands, while letting her legs dangle. They are clad in black nylon tights with her fitting black skirt covering the upper half of her thighs. As soon as she is aware of him, she sobers up and returns a friendly greeting. The two young men have also swivelled towards him: Rahul with his short black hair and regular dark features and Alastair, short strawberry blonde hair and a three-day stubble of a slightly darker hue around his pale square face.

'I actually wanted a word with Teresa', he says, 'but she is giving her seminar, isn´t she? I´ll see her after the lunch break, then. I am off to a meeting, now.'

After he has walked off and with the sound of his steps fading, Sabrina says with marked formality:

'Thank you for your assistance, Alastair. May I treat you to a cup of coffee?'

'Okay', Alastair replies, nonchalantly. 'I could use a break.'

'Let´s go to the cafeteria', Sabrina suggests. 'Their coffee tastes better, and they sell croissants. I haven´t had any breakfast, yet.'

Alastair accepted her proposal on impulse, which he now almost regrets. He is aware that Teresa wouldn´t be happy if she knew. Anyway, he would like to know more about this woman. As yet, there has never been any time or opportunity for a longer chat. When she came to see him in his office earlier on, she asked for his advice on a matter relating to her thesis, and they were having an interesting discussion. That´s what it should be like on a research team. And there is nothing wrong about taking a coffee break with this colleague, now, either.

The cafeteria is on the ground floor on the opposite side of the courtyard. While crossing over, he asks her a few follow-up questions. Then he pushes the entrance door open and gallantly lets her take the lead.

At this time of day only a few students are sitting at the tables with a cup and some documents or a laptop in front of them. As Sabrina and Alastair are the only customers, they proceed along the counter in no time and sit down at a table for two at one of the large shop windows: Sabrina with her croissant and a cup of coffee, Alastair, who is not hungry, with his cup of coffee.

'Do you miss England?' asks Sabrina.

'No, mostly not', Alastair answers curtly. 'Just the short distances to the sea no matter where you are.'

Why is he so unsociable, now? Sabrina wonders. Is he already sorry for joining me here? Or have I touched a soft spot? Wanting to know more, she decides to dig deeper.

'Where did you grow up?' she asks.

Although Alastair does not like talking about his family, he pulls himself together and elaborates:

'In Richmond just to the west of London, in a beautiful detached house, a Victorian villa. It was my grandfather's property. He co-owned a small shipyard. But my father did not follow in his footsteps. He became a bank manager, and my mother is a lawyer. Besides, she is an excellent piano player. It is to her that I owe my love of music', he says lost in thought. I order to tide over any suspicion that he might be sentimental he adds matter-of-factly:

'Of course, I attended a private school. – And what about you?'

'I was at a grammar school – a *Gymnasium* – in Munich', Sabrina recounts. 'My parents are doctors. My father is a surgeon and my mother a neurologist. Both are luminaries in their respective fields. They would have liked me to study medicine, too. But I did not reach the required marks.'

She stops and smiles archly, thus indicating that she was not particularly sad about this.

'It was not just because of the marks, though,' she continues. 'It might sound strange, but not meeting the requirements finally set me free to do something else. You see, my parents worked really long hours. My brother and me, we were basically raised by our grandparents. At home they talked shop all the time. After graduating from school, I just wanted to leave home, leave Munich. Meanwhile, it is not only my parents. My brother is training to become a consultant, too. — And why didn´t you stay in England? I liked it there. I spent my year abroad in Liverpool studying at the University.'

Due to Sabrina´s frankness Alastair´s own reluctance has melted. She has struck a chord which has made him willing to reciprocate.

'For similar reasons. I wanted to get to know another country, a different culture', he elaborates. 'While I was at school I wasn´t much interested in politics. We were well-off. I had all you could wish for. But when I started studying at Cambridge, I got in touch with independent-minded people. It was during the final years of Margaret Thatcher´s rule, the controversy about the poll tax. Only then did I understand how much her policies had changed the country and what the consequences were for the British workers: the decline of the industrial areas in the Midlands and above all in the North. From then on, my father and I argued when I was at home. After some time, however, I realized that it was pointless. I had become estranged from my parents. Their lifestyle was disagreeable to me. That's why I applied for postdoc positions outside of Britain, as well. — Why did you study in Liverpool of all places?'

'I was thrilled by what I heard about it', Sabrina explains. 'And I wanted to upset my parents a bit. Their daughter spending her year abroad there was incompatible with their social status.'

She laughs merrily.

'They associated the place at once with poverty, crime and hooligans', she continues. 'Of course, this wasn't the whole story. I enjoyed university life there. Nor did the town live up to its reputation. Things had already started to improve. Besides, such a seaport is exciting. The gate to the wide world.'

Alastair has listened with bright eyes. She seems to feel the magic of the sea and the pull of its vast horizons, too.

'And it's the city of the Beatles', Sabrina continues.

'The Beatles?' Alastair asks enthusiastically. 'You like their music?'

'Yes. Of course, the songs are classics. I used to play them a lot on the gramophone. I like the lyrics and the sound. They radiate the spirit of the 60s and 70s. Wild years, indeed. — Meanwhile, I have developed a love for R&B: Mariah Carey, Alicia Keys, Rihanna, Beyoncé, …'.

'Do you play an instrument yourself?'

'Yes', Sabrina relates. 'The guitar, but not particularly well. I am quite proud of my voice, though. I had singing lessons, and I even performed as the singer of a band for some time. We did gigs in the area around Munich. What about you? You said you were inspired by your mother.'

Alastair pauses, apparently lost in thought again. Then he says dreamily.

'Naturally, I had piano lessons, but my favourite instrument is the guitar. For a while I played a lot of blues. Do you know Jimi Hendrix? His music is divine. Of course, I am lightyears away from his art. I should resume practising every day. It is relaxing, as well. An entirely different world.'

He looks out of the window across the courtyard. Then as if brought down to earth.

'Oh, isn´t this Fatima?' With a jerk of his head he indicates the direction of the entrance door to the building opposite. A slim and not very tall woman in a knee-length beige coat is about to push it open. Her long dark hair reaches down to her shoulder blades.'

'Yes', Sabrina replies drily. 'She has just passed by.'

She glances at Alastair´s coffee cup. It is empty. He seems suddenly restless.

'Shall we?' she asks him. 'It´s lunchtime, soon.'

'All right', he says briskly, pushes back his chair and gets up.

Almost silently, they head back to their faculty building.

Teething troubles

It takes a while until everyone has left the room. As always, the student who gave the presentation would like to know about Teresa's first impressions. Another student asks a follow-up question and a particularly eager one wants her to recommend further reading. Thus, it is shortly before twelve, when she heads back to her office. There is still plenty of time. She arranged with her colleagues to have lunch together in the canteen at twelve thirty. While she strides through the familiar halls and corridors, moments from the seminar flash through her mind: remarkable details from the presentation, students' comments, some exchanges from their discussion.

After turning into their corridor, she stops by Mrs Lohr, who has a message from Professor Feldmann. He would like to have a word in the early afternoon. So she would have to make sure not to stay out at lunch too long. Her office is locked, which means that Fatima is not there, yet. She leaves the door open, sits down in front of her desk and leans her bag on the table leg to her left. She must remember the appointment with Professor Feldmann in the afternoon. To unburden her mind, she makes a note in her diary. An organizational matter surely, she thinks. He is a good boss. She likes him, nay, holds him in high esteem. He feels responsible for his staff, treats them as human beings and considers it his duty to provide an environment where they can make the most of their talents and abilities.

She thinks herself back to her beginnings as a doctoral candidate, when her usual anxiety became even worse, because she took her duties so seriously, because she wanted to do such a good job. Mrs Lohr was very important to her, then. When they talked in her office the tightness within her soon eased, and her muscles relaxed while the conversation took a more personal direction. Never would she forget, how much this meant to her.

It was thanks to her and also to Professor Feldmann that she settled in fast and found her bearings. He was somehow like a father but more distant. Always kind and responsive, though, when she needed his advice. When she felt that she was at a dead end with her work, she could draw inspiration and strength from their discussions. In his graduate seminars he shared his treasures of knowledge and his insights with them. She left each session feeling that she had learned something, that an as yet elusive aspect had become more concrete or that a subject was illuminated from a new angle. Perhaps now that her teething troubles were over, she could admit this, that back then she was almost a little in love with him. Was she? He understood. He had a similar background: lower middle-class, Catholic, conservative. Anyway, she would have liked a father like him, a father who radiated kindness. Her own father had been very strict. Regardless if it was her behaviour at home or her performance at school, it was never really good enough. She remembers her gnawing self-doubts. Only here as a member of Professor Feldmann's staff could she gain more confidence.

And then she met Alastair. Like her he obtained a postdoc position with the newly established collaborative research centre. She smiles dreamily, by now almost drowsing, when the sound of voices reaches her ear. Her colleagues are coming to pick her up. While Fatima enters with a cheerful *Hello Teresa*, Alastair remains leaning against the door frame.

'What about lunch, Resa?' he asks.

'In a second', she replies smiling at him, then starts digging in her bag for her purse. When she reaches the door, Alastair puts an arm around her shoulders and kisses her cheek. She beams at him. Sabrina and Rahul are waiting further down the corridor in front of the staircase. With Fatima and Alastair by her side she catches up with them.

The party

Professor Jakub Feldmann is standing in a circle of his colleagues in the seminar room, which has been festively decorated for the party. He only listens with half an ear to their sophisticated professional discussion while looking around.

His research staff – he likes to call them his team – are sitting around the end of the long table tucking into their desserts: Alastair Collins, one of the postdocs, at the head of the table, the doctoral candidates Sabrina Kühnel and Fatima Özdil on one side and the postdocs Teresa Rinaldi and Rahul Sabharwal opposite with his assistant Maximilian Schneider between them.

They are focused on eating as much as on their research, Jakub thinks with a fatherly smile, not a little amused. Now, he hears Alastair´s tenor voice. It wafts across to him over the hum of conversation like a solo instrument above the orchestra. From his position at the head of the table he entertains the others as he often does. There is a chorus of laughter. Teresa and Sabrina, the two young women next to him, look at him admiringly.

Only Maximilian, Sabrina and Teresa were born in Germany. Teresa´s father immigrated as a guest worker from Italy, though. Alastair is English, Rahul has roots in India and Fatima in Turkey. He himself emigrated from Poland ten years ago. Some of his colleagues have a migratory background, too. Half the world in one room. Meanwhile, he has learned a lot about other cultures.

'Daddy?' – His seven-year-old daughter Anna tugs at his sleeve. Jakub jumps. He has been lost in thought and during a party of all places.

'We are going home, Daddy.'

He looks down smiling at her and offers her his hand. Then he leads her gently to the open door behind which his wife Ela and their nine-year-old son Leo are waiting.

'I hope it won't get very late. As I am the big boss I have to stay on till everyone else has left', he says smiling apologetically at Ela.

‚It's alright', Ela replies and leans towards him to give him a little peck on the cheek.

'See you later.'

Jakub looks after them until they have disappeared behind the glass door to the staircase. Then he turns and once more lets his eye wander. The party has been a success. They have all contributed. Someone has cast a spell on the plain old seminar room. It is utterly transformed, decorated with garlands and balloons, flowers on the table. The buffet has been marvellous. Salads, different kinds of quiche, bowls with cut raw vegetables, desserts. Much of it self-made.

He invited the professors and those of their staff involved in the collaborative research center. It is a cherished tradition to celebrate the extension of a project together, which is tantamount to a recognition of the high quality of their work, after all. Besides, parties are an opportunity to get to know each other.

By now, however, everyone has retreated to their comfort zones. The professors stand together in a circle, their research staffs have formed small groups of their own and the research assistants and secretaries are sitting by themselves, too. He shrugs. You can´t make them mix, he thinks, and gathers himself together. It´s time to touch glasses with his team. He walks over to the buffet to fill a glass with champagne. Then he crosses the room to join them at their end of the table.

*

After a period of silence dedicated to the pleasure of eating their desserts, a new conversation sets in among Professor Feldmann´s staff, while Maximilian and Rahul are still enjoying their refills.

'Who is this Tiramisu from?' asks Maximilian. 'You, Ali?'

'No, it´s Teresa`s', says Alastair proudly.

Maximilian turns towards her and declares solemnly:

'Teresa, this is the best Tiramisu I´ve ever had.'

Teresa laughs, then says:

'You exaggerate! But thanks, anyway. I am glad you´ve enjoyed it.'

Leaning back with a sigh expressive of deep satisfaction, Maximilian remarks:

'Now, we have been really decadent, at least Rahul and me.'

Putting one hand on his stomach, Rahul leans back, as well and joins in:

'I absolutely agree.'

And he adds ironically: 'It's been western decadence all over. — In fact, this label does not apply to the Germans I have met so far. They work all day, often till late in the evening. And if they celebrate, they are really civilized.'

'Good point', Sabrina complains half joking. 'It's really boring with you all. You are terribly prudish.'

'O, yeah!' Maximilan chimes in. 'Drugs, sex and rock 'n' roll. That would be great! But sadly, we can't afford to have affairs or to go on a bender every weekend. When we are not at work, we do sports to keep fit for work. We shop for food, prepare an evening meal and watch the news while eating. On Sunday evenings we sit at home glued to another sequel of *Crime Scene*.'

'I knew some people in Cambridge who were really wild', Alastair remembers. 'Burnt the candle at both ends. But then it is hard to get your act together in the run-up to exams. If you don't, you can forget your career. Life's no joy without a well-paid job. Living from day to day, not knowing how to make ends meet.'

'You don't have to go to such extremes', Sabrina remarks. 'But don't we live in a free country? We should enjoy this more instead of letting ourselves be locked in so much. When I was in England during my year abroad, I used to know people who tried things out, not least with regard to their sexuality. If they were attracted by men or by women or maybe even both … that kind of thing. You got along well in your circle of friends. There were no steady relationships, but why not make love with each other at the end of a nice evening together? The next morning each was free to go their own way.'

'Really? Sex without love? Not for me', Teresa calls out in protest.

'Does it always have to be romantic, absolute love? Maybe there is no one and only', Sabrina elaborates her gaze fixed on Teresa. 'Why not free love based on affection between good friends instead?' she goes on, now turning to Alastair.

The latter lowers his head, but not in embarrassment. Something has caught his eye. With caution, he reaches for her forearm lying loosely next to her empty dessert bowl and with his thumb and forefinger picks a long, blond, curly hair from the sleeve of her black top. There seems to be great tenderness in the gesture.

'A hair', he says, holds it up for everyone to see and then drops it beside the table.

'Yours', he says looking at Sabrina.

'Thank you', Sabrina replies in her silky voice smiling at Alastair.

Teresa struggles to keep down the anger and jealousy rising in her throat. As Alastair has already started to continue speaking as if nothing happened, she swallows her emotions and reconsiders.

'It is true that it´s important for many young people in my country to be free', Alastair says. 'At school, at university and at work they have to pull themselves together. But in their spare time they don´t want any rules. At least they insist on free choice, in love as much as in the pub.'

He smiles sarcastically.

'Now', Teresa interjects with a visible effort to control herself. 'I don´t think that free love works. People just end up hurting each other.'

'Of course, some of them go too far', Alastair replies reassuringly. 'I don´t fancy such excesses, not any more, at least.'

A hint of a grin somewhere between self-irony and regret shows in his face

'But I sometimes miss going to a pub after work', he adds. 'Having a beer together, talking, laughing and flirting a little. Here, everyone is so earnest. At least in our department. Of course, this is not all bad.'

He looks at Teresa tenderly and also a bit wistfully.

Now, Fatima turns to Alastair, cushioning her indignation with a humorous undertone:

'You miss flirting? You are not serious, are you? After all, you are in a steady relationship. Remember?'

There is an edge to Sabrina´s voice when she comments:

'Isn´t it more dangerous for a relationship, if a man is not allowed to look at other women or vice versa? So much restraint increases the temptation to really cross the boundaries and start an affair.'

'If I were Alastair, I would be in paradise, not in prison', Maximilian says to calm the waves.

'Don´t worry', says Alastair apologetically to Teresa. 'I am just a bit nostalgic. There is a time and a season for everything, and I am really happy as it is.'

He puts his arm around her and kisses her tenderly on her lips.

Their colleagues cheer.

'Finally. Good job!' Rahul exclaims. 'After all, you have chosen each other. In my culture the parents often have a say in who is an appropriate partner. Some interfere more, others not so much. Above all they want their sons and daughters-in-law to be from families of similar social status. Religion is important, too. Even your affiliation to a caste can still play a role. And if you are homosexual you´d better not make this public.'

'I have relatives who travelled to Turkey with their kids to marry them off there', Fatima recounts. 'To a partner who has not been spoiled by western culture. I´m sure my parents would prefer my future husband to be from a Turkish family, not least because of our relatives. My uncle is very conservative. He always tells me not to bring shame on our family. This means that I am not supposed to go on dates, not to speak of going out with German men. As to flirting – I have never dared, but since I moved to another town, I feel much freer. It would be nice to have a boy-friend, but I don't want to marry, yet. Not for a long time. On the one hand my parents are proud of me, a university graduate, and they understand that my work as a researcher is very important to me. But like all Turkish parents they are going to ask when I'll marry and have kids sometime soon.'

'Lucky we, who are not tied to such a tradition', Maximilian remarks. 'We really don't have anything to complain about.'

*

Meanwhile Professor Dr Jakub Feldmann has approached. He takes his seat next to Rahul. As they have fallen silent, he lifts his glass and says:

'Let's raise our glasses. To you and your excellent work.'

It takes a while until each has clicked glasses with everybody else. There is laughter, because it is not easy not to get in each other's way. When it is Jakub's turn to lock eyes with Rahul while their glasses touch, he is once again inadvertently spell-bound.

'What was it like in Poland, Professor Feldmann?' Sabrina asks suddenly. 'Was free love on the table, too?'

Her voice reaches him from far away, and it takes a moment until he has rallied and caught up. What a question! She might have observed him. Is she trying to find a sore spot? She might just be checking out how far she can go, though. There has always been something provocative about her, he tells himself reassuringly. Aware that all eyes are turned towards him, he decides for a general, matter-of-fact answer.

'In Poland people tend to be very conservative', he says. 'During the People's Republic, when the country was under a communist dictatorship, the system was atheist. Nonetheless, many considered the Catholic Church their spiritual home. Thus, it remained influential. Based on their humanist ideals it even advocated political reforms and was a sanctuary for dissidents.

My family has always stuck to their Catholic faith in private. Only when I started university, did I get in touch with more liberal circles. I enjoyed not being under surveillance so much, any more. You could date someone – he smiles – without thinking of the future, just because you wanted to go out and have fun.

We weren't as free as you are today, especially in Germany, but freer than in rural areas in Poland. There, it is much more important what the family thinks. Perhaps you can't ever escape from that.'

A secret

When Jakub leaves the building, it is shortly after midnight. If he hurries, he'll catch the 0:20 tram. He sets out at a rapid pace crossing the square, then turns round the corner by the stationer's and walks straight on to Emperor's Avenue, at times falling into a trot. From here the Timber Market is only a few metres to the right. When he arrives, the number three is just approaching from the Southern Gate. At this time of the day on weekdays there is no lack of free seats so that he has a whole row to himself. He is tired, but content. The party was a success. What a great atmosphere. Everyone in high spirits, and they deserved it. Nice work. This is what I like about my job. Working with such talented young people. And each of them is unique.

Alastair Collins is the star of the team. PhD from Cambridge. An impressive track record already at his young age. He has great future prospects. Besides, he is charming and has a delightful sense of humour. A talent to entertain and make other people laugh. With his three-day reddish stubble, he appears a bit roguish.

Teresa Rinaldi is completely different. She is an excellent researcher in her own way. Easily overlooked though because she is so very quiet. Meanwhile, however, everyone knows that it is worth listening when she speaks up. She is highly esteemed. How strange that they are a couple, Teresa and Alastair, with him so lively and bright and her, by contrast, so sober and modest but with such great potential. And how she adores him. I hope, he won't let her down.

And what about Sabrina Kühnel? At times it seems that she has a hidden agenda. When I locked eyes with Rahul while toasting the extension of the project. She can´t possibly have noticed. With her question she surely struck a nerve, presumably without being aware in what regard exactly.

He is so preoccupied that he has lost track of the stops. The running ribbon of red letters under the roof of the tram tells him that indeed, he has to get off at the next one. He waits in front of the back doors until the tram comes to a halt and they open. From here to his flat it is only a few minutes on foot.

Where was he? Clinking glasses. A pair of enchanting dark-brown eyes. Rahul Sabharwal. This handsome young man, whose manner is sometimes so formal that he is dignity personified, should actually like him? Or is this wishful thinking?

He seems mature for his age. Perhaps because he has seen so much of the world. Born in Delhi, childhood and youth in Washington as the son of a high-ranking diplomat. Privileged upbringing no doubt. There is something genteel about him. His ancestors Brahmins, probably of the highest order. Indian nobility, anyway. And he has brains and talent, as well. A PhD from the University of California, Berkeley. His dark eyes. Sometimes full of melancholia, as if he has had to go through some painful experience. No wonder, always standing out as the stranger in foreign lands. Am I in love? Maybe, but I must not indulge in it.

With this resolution he opens the front door and mounts the stairs to his flat on the second floor. While hanging up his coat on the wardrobe in the corridor, he is unable to escape the long mirror on the wall next to it. As always, his gaze is captured by the reflection of his person rising from its depths, his powerfully built body, his broad shoulders. He would have liked to be a bit taller and more athletic. With a sigh he notices the beginnings of a paunch, which, however, is concealed very well by his brown Tweed jacket. His eyes have the colour of corn flowers in a field of wheat in summer, someone once told him. He smiles his broad smile, which makes his face look round like the moon. Ela´s words. But there are also silvery strands among the originally golden blonde thatch, especially at the temples and in his forelock, too. He has grown old. … Rubbish. It´s just been a long day.

He turns away from the mirror and first parks his briefcase in his study, then uses the bathroom where he gets ready for bed. On his way to the bedroom he checks on the children. Both are fast asleep, each on their side of the folding screen dividing the room in two halves. Then he pads into the bedroom he shares with Ela. As the moon shines through the slits in the shutters, he can do without switching on the light. As cautiously as possible he lies down on his back on his side of the bed. By no means does he want to disturb her. But now, she mumbles something in her sleep, and after a subsequent turn of her head and shoulder her arm comes to lean on his chest as if reaching out to him. Overcome by tenderness, he props himself up a little and brushes her palm gently with his lips.

'Ela', he mouths.

Chapter Two

September 1999 - February 2000

The morning after

Teresa is standing in front of the sink in the ladies' room at the end of the corridor and gazes into the mirror. Her face looks pale and drawn. Could she be pregnant? Or was it because she drank more than usual last night? While sitting at her desk in front of the computer screen earlier on, she suddenly felt queasy. She tries to calculate how much time has passed since her last period, but gets mixed up. She can't think clearly at the moment. The pressure in her head, which she has had since she woke up, has increased. She collects some water in her palm and spreads it on her forehead, her cheeks and her neck. Then she lifts her shoulders almost to her earlobes a few times to ease the tension in her upper back.

With a baby everything would change. Of course, she would be happy. It would be their child. On the other hand, she would so much like to go on working, at least till her contract terminates. Maybe it'll even be renewed. Despite the self-doubt racking her time and again she knows that her qualifications are excellent. This would not be of much help though. When she paused for longer than a year, it would be almost impossible to catch up. She might never be taken on as a researcher, any more, although she has always believed this to be her vocation. And besides, it is what she has in common with Alastair.

She was delighted when she heard that their research project would be extended. And she enjoyed celebrating this, though as a rule she doesn´t like the behaviour that goes with the lower inhibition level due to too much alcohol, not to speak of the noise. People suddenly only engage in banter or turn utterly silly. It wearies her, when they are so exuberant.

But Alastair is completely in his element, then. He likes being in the limelight. Sabrina knows this perfectly well and uses it to her advantage. She is quick-witted like him, and he plays along. In general, Teresa doesn´t mind, but when he picked this hair from her sleeve, yesterday, it really stung and does again now that she thinks of it. And it still makes her furious. Why is he so charming to Sabrina? With her being so easy-going and self-confident, maybe she would be the better match. But when he looked at her, Teresa, and kissed her in front of everybody, she was so relieved and happy! He does love her, after all.

And Sabrina? What does she want from him? Everyone knows that they are together. And they have all known this before yesterday.

She jumps when the door opens and Sabrina´s image appears in the mirror behind her own pale face.

'Are you alright?' Sabrina asks. Then after a pause she adds:

'Or are you not feeling well?'

'I am fine, thank you', Teresa answers. 'A little hung over, perhaps.'

After Sabrina has locked herself in one of the cubicles, she hears the door fall shut behind Teresa.

Hung over. Ha, ha, when she has hardly had anything to drink, she thinks with a twinge of sarcasm.

Is she pregnant? A love child!? she ruminates with mixed feelings. No doubt. After all, family planning shouldn't be a problem anymore, today.

A heart-to-heart talk

After work Teresa and Fatima head for the inner city. Recently, the latter tried on a skirt at the *Galleria* department store but was unsure whether it really suited her. So she asked Teresa to go along with her sometime soon. When her colleague was unwell in the morning, Fatima offered to postpone their shopping tour, but Teresa insisted on following it through. Now, Fatima has just bought the skirt, and satisfied with the bargain she suggests a break in the *Café in the Meadows*. After the waitress has served each of them her can of tea, Teresa braces herself and says:

'Maybe I am pregnant. My period should have set in three days ago, and this morning I felt sick.'

'How lovely!' says Fatima smiling, but after searching Teresa's face she adds compassionately:

'Or aren't you happy?'

'I don't know', Teresa replies honestly and elaborates:

'I don't feel ready, yet. I would have liked to wait, at least till my contract runs out.'

Fatima wears her heart on her sleeve, and Teresa pre-empts her:

'… Yes, I know. … But the pill did not agree with me.'

'Have you told Alastair?' Fatima asks.

Teresa shakes her head.

'I haven´t done the test, yet. It might still turn out negative', she says. 'I just had more champagne than usual yesterday. That might be all.'

Fatima is concerned:

'Would Alastair be happy about this?'

'I think so', says Teresa anxiously, 'but I am not sure. We haven´t talked about children. So far, we have mainly identified with our work. A baby would turn everything upside down, of course.'

'Yes. You would be staying at home with the baby for the time being', she reflects. 'But once they go to nursery school, there will be opportunities to resume your work', she adds noticing Teresa´s unhappy face.

'Three years seems like ages', says Teresa despondently. 'It´ll be hard to catch up after such a long time. I wonder if I would have a chance at all.'

'No need to worry, now. Perhaps, you are not pregnant after all', says Fatima trying to raise her spirits.

'Hopefully', Teresa replies miserably. 'I would like to marry first.'

'Marry?' Fatima is surprised. 'I thought that this isn´t important any more in Germany today, is it?'

'Alastair says so, too', Teresa admits. 'He ´d prefer not to marry. He says that the partners would start to take each other for granted, and the love between them would cool down sooner. I don't know. But my parents have very strong views on this. Although they have been living in Germany for quite a long time, they don't really have contacts outside their circle of Italian families, who are all orthodox Catholics, at least the guest worker generation. They and our relatives in Naples reinforce my parents' conservatism.'

'This sounds familiar', Fatima concurs. 'My parents would tell me off, too, although they are not such strict Muslims themselves.'

'Maybe we should take courage and live our own lives, hard as it is to alienate one's parents', says Teresa firmly. 'Anyway, there is something else which I am even more scared of.'

'What is it?' Fatima enquires worriedly

'You'll think my imagination is running away with me', says Teresa evasively.

'Please, tell me all', Fatima demands. 'That's what friends are for. Listening. I'll give you a shout, if you hallucinate.'

'Sabrina and Alastair', Teresa blurts out. 'I am jealous. I am afraid she is going to take him away from me.'

Fatima slaps her forehead with her palm:

'I have totally forgotten. On my way across the courtyard yesterday. I am not quite sure, but I had a glimpse of two people sitting at a table at the window in the cafeteria. They looked like them.'

Teresa stares into space gloomily:

'This must have been during my seminar', she says shaking her head. 'It wouldn't help to put him in chains, though. He needs other people more than I do. Still, it hurts terribly. Did you watch them yesterday night during our discussion?'

'The hair, on her sleeve?' asks Fatima.

'Yes', she sighs dejectedly. 'Probably, you can never be sure.'

And with a brave smile she adds:

'Thank you for listening. It's been good talking to you.'

'You are very welcome', Fatima says warmly.

She calls the waitress and pays for both of them. Then they walk the short distance to Duke Square where they get onto different trams. Teresa is going to spend the night in her room in the shared flat and will be buying a pregnancy test at a pharmacy on her way there.

During the night she sleeps only fitfully. When she wakes up, she tosses and turns till she falls asleep again. Now, it is four in the morning. The room is brightened by the moonlight coming in through a gap between the curtains. Again, she lies awake for a long time, but must have nodded off once more, because when the alarm clock rings at a quarter to seven, it is as if she is ripped out of a deep sleep. She permits herself to drowse trying to re-enter this safe space of forgetfulness where she has just been. But there is no going back. So she snaps out of her wistfulness and props herself up in bed. There is a slight queasiness again, or does she imagine it?

She pads into the bathroom and takes the pregnancy test. Unambiguously positive. At least she knows for sure, now.

Certainty

In the evening of the next day Alastair and Teresa ride their bikes back home from work. They are heading for the quarter in the north of the city where Alastair´s apartment is located just a few blocks away from Teresa´s shared flat. Teresa loves to pass by the fanciful art nouveau villas, each house a small individually designed palace. They ride along the tree-lined roads, under the vaults made of the foliage of large old plane trees. Today even more than usual she enjoys the mild September afternoon air stroking her skin. Though it almost takes half an hour, it has never seemed a long way to her.

They stop at a nearby supermarket to buy some provisions and in particular ingredients for the curry Alastair wants to cook for their dinner. On their arrival in his flat he puts on an Eric Clapton CD, which both of them like, and Teresa helps him cut the vegetables and prepare the spices. Then she leaves the final preparations to him and lays the small table in the kitchen. While the curry simmers on the stove, she crosses the living room and steps out on the terrace where she sits down on the bench in front of the garden table pondering for the umpteenth time today how she is going to tell him. In any case she'll wait till after dinner.

With the sun blocked out by the surrounding houses, the air has cooled fast, or is it her nervousness? Feeling more and more cold she returns to the living room closing the door behind her.

The living room has been furnished tastefully with a selection of beautiful pieces that nonetheless go well together. On the side of the terrace there is a sofa and two matching armchairs around a coffee table. Alastair's guitar leans in the corner next to the lamp. On the wall opposite the sofa the television towers above the hi-fi system. Further to the right in front of the window is Alastair's desk made of a dark reddish wood, and on the adjoining wall a shelf well-stocked with books and files extends as far as the door.

As always, she is amused by the work surface of the desk being wiped clean of everything except the computer screen and a stack of document trays. It is as if he never used it. Instead, he is just very well organised. It is paramount to him that everything is in its place.

As always, the enlarged black-and-white photo of a sailing boat catches her eye. It is leaning to one side in the wind and its bow is lifted in the face of the oncoming wave. An elderly man with sideburns wearing a captain's hat is sitting at the tiller, while a youth looks after the sails. They are Alastair and his grandfather during their last regatta. When he died soon after, his grandson mourned him for a long time. Thinking about this now, Teresa feels very sad herself.

'Dinner is ready!' It is Alastair who summons her back to the present.

Teresa enters the kitchen smiling at him and communicating her pleasure at how good the curry looks and smells. It is not unusual for her to decline the glass of red wine Alastair offers her. While they are eating and later clearing the table and washing up, they only exchange a few observations and information which has accumulated during the day.

When they finally sit next to each other on the sofa, it is Alastair who makes a start. He puts his arm around Teresa and encourages her to lean against him.

'Are you all right?' he asks. 'I have been wondering for two days, now. You are even quieter than usual.'

'I am pregnant', she breathes just audibly. 'I took the test this morning.'

He takes her in his arms and kisses her gently on the forehead.

'And? What do you think?' she asks looking at him quizzically and feeling anxious all the while.

'I did not really expect it', Alastair replies. 'But I am happy, of course', he adds smiling and kissing her on her lips.

Now that they are talking with each other and making plans for the future, the weight in Teresa's chest gradually dissolves, and Alastair has soon regained her trust. He is so charming and speaks so warmly that her spirits lift until she is radiant with joy.

When they have switched off the lights late in the evening and agreed to go to sleep, Teresa is aware that she has not broached the issue of Sabrina. Nor have they talked about marriage.

The farewell party

It is six months later on Teresa´s last day at work before her maternity leave. In mid-afternoon her colleagues have gathered in the small conference room opposite the staff kitchen to give her a farewell party. Professor Jakub Feldmann treats them to the drinks. There is champagne and some bottles of beer and, for the non-drinkers, orange juice and water. Two tables have been pushed together on which assorted quiches and some self-made salads are spread.

Jakub has just entered the room. He apologizes for being late because of an important phone call and sits down at the free head of the table next to Rahul on one side and Mrs Lohr on the other. Opposite him he recognizes Alastair with Teresa and Sabrina next to him. From the corner of his eye he notices Rahul pouring him some champagne. As their conversation has flagged, anyway, he lifts his glass to propose a toast.

'Here is to Teresa and the baby. All the very best for you two — no, the three of you, of course,' he says looking warmly first at Teresa, then at Alastair and smiling his fatherly smile. For a while they are all busy clicking glasses with Teresa and Alastair.

Sabrina is unable to refrain from teasing Teresa.

'What about half a glass of champagne, Teresa?' she asks. 'It´s your party, after all!'

Teresa, who is holding a champagne glass of water in her hand, replies curtly:

'No, thank you.'

Mrs Lohr supports her not without an edge in her voice:

'Teresa is right. Even small amounts of alcohol could do harm to the baby.'

Fatima comes to her defence, too. Putting an arm around her, she says warmly:

'I´ll miss you, Teresa. You are the good angel of the team.'

Maximilian joins in:

'I trust you´ll be around. Why not pop by once in a while for a chat and a cup of tea? I´m sure, you´d like to keep in touch.'

'Of course, you are always welcome', Jakub confirms. 'Perhaps there will be an opportunity for you to get on board again after your parental leave.'

'This would be great', Teresa replies self-consciously. 'It won´t be easy, though. My parents don´t live close by. Besides, they could not leave their shop on weekdays. And Alastair´s parents are in England. The university has a nursery for children from the age of two. But at that age they are still so small, aren´t they? There is only a limited number of places, anyway.'

'You could take turns looking after the baby', Sabrina suggests breezily. 'Why doesn´t Alastair take paternity leave when the baby is one or two? I can well imagine it.'

She smirks at Alastair.

Fatima turns to Teresa and puts her hand on hers: 'Don´t worry about the future, now. Why not just be happy about the baby and look forward to holding him in your arms.'

Teresa gives her a forced smile and then includes them all in her gaze:

'It will be strange not to be here every day any more. I´ll miss you and my work', she says.

'You can use your free time to go shopping', Sabrina suggests. 'Or do you already have all the baby clothes?'

Rahul looks at Jakub with a tortured smile on his face. Jakub understands and opens his mouth to say something. But Alastair is faster:

'Naturally, we´ll do this together.' He smiles at Teresa and puts his arm around her.

Now Jakub suggests:

'I´ll ask my wife, if she has any baby clothes left. May I give you her phone number? She might have handed them down to her sister, though.'

Teresa reaches for the *Post It* block, which has been left in the middle of the table, writes down her phone number and pushes the note across to Rahul who relays it to his boss with a smile. At that moment their eyes meet for a split second causing a shiver to run down Jakub´s spine.

'Thank you', he says coolly, while pulling his purse out of his pocket and tucking the slip of paper in with the banknotes.

'By the way', he announces in a cheerful tone of voice. 'You are welcome to help yourselves to the buffet.'

While Teresa and Alastair set off for home, their colleagues carry the plates, cutlery and glasses into the staff kitchen. Fatima and Maximilian have volunteered to fill the dish washer. Thus, Rahul and Sabrina remain behind in the conference room packing their empty dishes into their bags.

It is Rahul who breaks the silence:

'You do have something against Teresa, don´t you?' he remarks.

Sabrina darts a challenging look at him.

'I can´t say that she doesn´t get on my nerves. So quiet and so modest. Always appropriate. It gets my hackles up.'

'From today you are rid of her. At least for a while', Rahul retorts coldly and scathingly.

'Give me a break', Sabrina protests. 'You do love her, then?'

'She is okay', says Rahul and looks her firmly in the eyes. 'But you are set on hurting her. That's not fair.'

'You are a noble person', she says half-mockingly brushing his shoulder with her hand while passing him on her way to the door.

Rahul is also one of those who always behave properly. What might be behind this sleek façade? she wonders. He stands up for Teresa, but he does not love her. Just like Professor Feldmann. He protects her in his role as her boss. He always acts professionally, and there is something fatherly in his manner. Towards all of us, though. He admires Teresa's work, and he likes her, too. Still, he is not in love with her. With Rahul perhaps? There seems to be a mutual understanding between them and also some strange tension. At the party while we drank to the success of the project. These gazes. Earlier on today, too. The *Post It*. Rahul did not write anything on it. She snickers. Everyone would have noticed. No. It was like Chinese Whispers. With a jubilant expression on her face she turns into the staircase.

Alone

When Teresa gets up, Alastair has already left for work. She brews herself a cup of tea and sits down at the kitchen table where a newspaper is spread.

Alastair has subscribed to it not least for the local news. He wants to know what's going on around him, what is on the minds of the people in his surroundings, what issues and problems they deal with. Teresa begins to read the headlines, but she isn't in the mood to immerse herself in a whole article. She is preoccupied with herself.

Yes, she did well to sleep in this morning. Her body demands it. It has a will of its own, now. When she senses little Georgie, she always wonders what he is doing – has he just moved a leg or an arm or turned around? She is not one, any more, but two. Her own life as such has lost its importance, she thinks during her turns of melancholia. Speaking with her parents on the phone, for example, it has struck her that they only think of her as Georgie's mother, now. They are so happy about the baby, their Giorgio, that they don't even mind that their daughter is not going to be married before his birth.

With Fatima it is similar. She means well, but in her opinion Teresa ought to be unconditionally happy, as if she didn't have any right to have doubts and wishes for herself. It seems as if the people around her set all their hopes on Georgie, as with him new and better times are going to break. Until then it is her sole role to carry him inside her. And it is her true destiny to be his mother.

So far she considered herself to be an independent being, making her own decisions. Thus, she became a researcher working on an exciting project with which she identified. In her dreams she would picture its likely progress, as yet indefinite, on a horizon where her own future lay concealed, as well.

She was used to obtaining recognition for measurable achievements: Marks, certificates, research papers. Now, however, she sees herself adored, even worshipped because she carries a little human being inside herself, who has raised great expectations. Apparently, it is her holy duty to dedicate her life entirely to him. This will require a kind of heroism she has never sought, and which she is afraid will lead her into an abyss of loneliness.

Her work was liberating, not least because her gender was unimportant. Her relationship with Alastair did not change this significantly. By becoming pregnant, however, she passed the threshold to the next age of a living being, that of a mother. Her child is now present in all her thoughts, decisions and plans. Nothing is for herself alone any more, and she will have to submit to a kind of dependence on others from which she believed to have liberated herself. Thus, it has been across the ages since prehistoric times. She is overcome by awe. It is not her due to put this law of nature into question, to rebel.

Nevertheless, she suddenly feels rebellious. Is it so selfish to go on dreaming of a future career? She thinks of Marie Curie, her heroine and role model. She and her husband, who was a famous physicist, too, shared in the childcare for their daughter. Sabrina had a point when she suggested that she and Alastair should take turns staying at home with the baby.

Sabrina. So wild, so confident, so free. Breezing through the corridors of the department like a gust of wind turning things upside down. And leaving a stab of pain in her wake. It still resonates in her heart. The hair at the party. Now that she is at home, Alastair can flirt with her unobserved. He does it in a characteristically ambiguous way so that what appears to be a friendly gesture might as well be seen as a loving one. And although on the threshold of tenderness one moment, he seems to be all indifferent the next. But only with others, not with her. Alastair – her great love. And he loves her, too. When they are by themselves, she is touched by how tender and attentive he is and by the efforts he puts in to make her happy. He is able to transform an ordinary evening into a festive occasion by cooking a delicious meal and playing some beautiful music. Only for the two of them.

The happiness in his voice when he talks about Georgie. She senses a twitch in her belly as if the baby heard his name. She puts the palm of her hand on the balloon-shaped swelling. Georgie, she mouths. After all, she does not have any reason to feel low. She must leave her insecurity, her anxiety, behind with her old life and look ahead bravely and optimistically. The sun rays coming in through the kitchen window warm her back. Puddles of light have formed on the table top and on the walls and fixtures. She is hungry. What about a croissant fresh from the bakers? she mumbles speaking both to herself and to Georgie. While she is at it, she can as well buy the loaf of bread they need. She rises and remains standing for a moment to balance herself. Then she fetches her coat, her purse and a shopping bag and steps out to meet the cold but sunny February day.

Chapter Three

July - October 2000

A visit

It is a sunny and very warm summer's day. In the faculty building, which is shielded from the sun by the foliage of big old plane trees, many windows and doors are open so that Jakub senses a refreshingly cool draft in the corridor while walking towards his office. When he recognizes Teresa, who just leaves Mrs Lohr's office, he is pleasantly surprised. She approaches him with the baby in a sling on her front, and he goes to meet her smiling and greeting her warmly.

'How are you?' he asks.

'Fine', she answers, but her face is pale. Alastair said that it was a difficult birth. She went into labour early, suffered wave on wave of excruciating pain for many hours until the child was actually born.

'You look tired', he remarks.

'Yes', she says. 'He does not sleep so very well at night. When he wakes up, he wants to be breastfed. That's okay, but when he has finished, he refuses to drop off to sleep again, at least in his own crib.'

Jakub bends down to have a closer look at the baby. To give him a better view of the little face, Teresa rearranges the baby sling.

'Hello Georgie', he says kindly. Georgie stares at him with his large eyes looking alarmed.

'What a cute little boy', Jakub says smiling at Teresa and at Alastair who has approached meanwhile and is standing next to her. Then he addresses the baby once more:

'Little man', he says in a soft voice. 'If you don´t let your Mummy and Daddy get more sleep, you´ll wear them out, soon'.

He turns to Teresa again and says reassuringly:

'It´s hard when they don´t sleep, but it´ll pass.'

And stretching out his hand for her to shake:

'I have to go back to work. It was nice seeing you. Remember to pop by from time to time.'

When he withdraws into his office, Alastair puts an arm around Teresa and asks:

'Would you like some tea?'

With Teresa nodding her assent, Rahul, who has meanwhile joined them, says:

'Good idea. Let´s have a cup of tea together.'

Alastair fills the electric kettle and prepares the cups. Maximilian and Teresa sit down at the table. The baby is lying in the crook of Teresa´s arm, now. He has fastened his eyes on Rahul, while moving his arms up and down and sucking his dummy from time to time.

When Alastair is about to put the cups before them on the table, Sabrina enters.

'Hello Teresa', she says breezily. 'How nice of you to come and see us. How are you?'

'Fine, thank you', Teresa replies, while Sabrina crosses over to the coffee machine.

While she pours herself a cup, Maximilian comes in.

'Hello, Teresa', he exclaims. 'I heard that something is going on here. Nice to see you.'

He bends down to the baby in its sling.

'Welcome on our team, Georgie', he says. 'Who of you does he take after?'

He peers at little Georgie's face.

'I would say that he has Teresa's brown eyes and hair and Alastair's features. Lucky baby. One day, you'll be as good-looking as him.'

Straightening up, he chuckles good-humouredly while Alastair boxes his shoulder in mock protest.

'Your baby has already become your rival', Sabrina remarks not without malice.

Georgie follows her with his eyes. While she is speaking, his arms move faster as if he senses her hostility.

Alastair puts an arm around Teresa:

'You see, Sabrina is still the same. Unable to refrain from teasing us.'

Sabrina, who has ignored the baby, says:

'Time to move on. I have to finish my literature survey. See you around.'

Balancing her cup of coffee in front of her, she leaves the kitchen.

'What's all this about', Maximilian asks shaking his head in disbelief. 'Jealousy?'

He gazes at Alastair with a grin on his face.

'Who knows?' Alastair replies ironically, grinning back.

Meanwhile, Georgie has turned his head and shoulders towards Teresa, and the soft noises he makes sound querulous. His little body has tensed.

'He is hungry', Teresa explains. 'I'll feed him here in the kitchen before I go.'

This is Maximilian and Rahul's clue to say their good-byes. Only Alastair remains sitting for a while before retreating into his office, too.

How strange to be here as a guest, Teresa thinks. Life at Professor Feldmann's chair has gone on without her. When she is at home, she can block this out. She has enough to do. Georgie takes up a lot of her time and besides, there are her household chores. Together they are her world, now. Due to the short nights she is often tired and worn-out during the day. Maybe breastfeeding Georgie has drained her of strength, too. She is glad not to have to work.

Presently, however, she is painfully aware of her loss. It was nice to see them, most of all Mrs Lohr, but also Professor Feldmann, Maximilian and Rahul, everyone but Sabrina who was her usual prickly self. For a while she and Georgie were in the limelight, which for once she quite enjoyed. But now that they went back to work, she feels excluded. As if they already didn't take her seriously any more as a colleague. She gazes wistfully at Georgie's little head and touches his downy, dark curls gently with her fingers, while he suckles weakly a few more times at her almost empty breast.

The breakdown

On a Friday morning in late October Rahul is already working in their shared office when Alastair comes in. On his way he stopped in the staff kitchen to pour himself a double espresso. Now he puts his cup next to the keyboard of his computer, sloughs off his shoulder bag and leans it against the leg of their desk on his side. With the reddish three-day stubble in his pale face and dark circles under his eyes he looks like a sailor who has just returned from a journey around the world. Rahul puts it more bluntly:

'You look like a zombie', he says.

'Thank you', Alastair replies deadpan. 'I just don't get enough sleep. Tonight, Georgie woke up around two a.m. I got up and fetched him for Teresa to feed. Afterwards it took him ages till he dropped off to sleep again. And when I was finally back in bed, I lay awake for a long time.'

'How is Teresa?' Rahul enquires.

'You do know her, don't you?' Alastair replies. 'She wants to be perfect all around. A perfect mother, a perfect housewife, and when Georgie is asleep, she reads up on her research topic. When she dozes off in the process, she is angry with herself. That's a bit too much.'

He forces a smile.

Rahul asks thoughtfully:

'And you don't have anyone who could support you now and then?'

'No, alas', Alastair sighs. 'Our parents don´t live around here, you know, but we are not lonely. With a baby you make new friends easily. We have met other families in our quarter. And there is a weekly parent-child-club which Teresa attends regularly. Fatima pops by sometimes.'

'Why don´t you hire a babysitter once in a while', Rahul suggests. 'When Georgie sleeps from eight to two, you could easily go to the cinema or on a stroll through the city treating yourselves to dinner some-where.'

'I´ve already suggested this', Alastair explains, 'but Teresa is too afraid to leave Georgie with a stranger. On the one hand I can understand her, and right now I do all I can for her and him. But she is so focused on him that it starts to frustrate me.'

'There is no way but to be patient', Rahul counsels. 'Give her some more time. Or — why not ask her about her fears? Try to find out what lies behind them.'

'This is easier said than done', Alastair sighs. And with a wry glance at Rahul:

'She knows what is best for Georgie.'

Then, he braces himself:

'Back to work', he says. 'I have to finish this data analysis, at last.'

*

After the lunch break Jakub is sitting in his office writing an e-mail. There is so much to organize these days. This morning he learned that Mrs Lohr was going to be on sick leave for a longer time. A disaster. He contacted the personnel department at once, hoping that he would get a replacement next week, at least a part-time one.

There is a knock at the door.

'Come in', Jakub calls mechanically and turns round. It is Rahul.

Jakub's heart misses a beat as always at unexpected encounters with him.

'Hello, Professor Feldmann. Can you spare a few minutes?' he asks.

'One second, please', Jakub replies in a daze. 'I'm almost done.'

He finishes writing his e-mail, then swivels his chair to face Rahul, who must have shut the door quietly in the meantime, and looks at him questioningly. Rahul starts to tell him what he learned from Alastair in the morning.

'Did your wife get in touch with Teresa as you offered during her farewell party?' he concludes.

Rahul gazes at him with such a piercing look that Jakub lowers his eyes. Hoping to gloss over his embarrassment, he swivels to his desk and reaches for his purse.

'The *Post It* note. Blimey, I've completely forgotten', he mumbles.

Despite his sense of foreboding, he is entirely caught off guard by what comes now:

'You like me', says Rahul passionately. 'I feel it.'

Jakub forces himself to stay calm and turns to face Rahul again.

'Yes, of course', he says. 'How is it possible not to, kind and smart as you are.'

His chest has tightened. Inwardly, he curses the locked door. But Rahul is relentless:

'I don't mean it that way. — It's that you love me as I love you.'

Jakub lowers his head. It's too hot in here. He pulls himself together and meets Rahul's gaze.

'Please, stop talking like that', he says with an effort. 'It is out of the question, above all here at your workplace. I am your supervisor, and I have a family.'

But Rahul ignores these words of warning. His emotions gush out of him like lava.

'Then you do love me!' he calls, deeply shaken. 'You repress your emotions, you have done it all your life! I know what this is like. This is not living! Of course, in Poland you didn't have much choice. But here in Germany society is much more open. In this city no-one cares if you walk hand in hand with a man.'

Jakub gets up and walks to the door.

'Calm down, please', he says, 'and for God's sake act as if this conversation has never taken place.'

He opens the door thus leaving Rahul no other option than to retreat to the corridor and hopefully return quietly to his room. Then, he himself walks back to his desk on wobbly legs. Mechanically, he takes Sabrina's essay out of his in-tray. She handed it in this morning. He starts reading, but troubled as he is, he is unable to concentrate. Again and again, he catches himself staring into space. Whenever he comes to, he has to reorient himself in the text. Finally, he concludes that it doesn't make sense to go on working, now. Today, he won't be the last to leave. He shuts down his computer, shoves the essay into his briefcase, puts on his coat and leaves the room. On passing the open doors of the staff members, he says a quick good-bye as if in a hurry and steps onto the staircase. Unusually early. They'll wonder what's going on.

An outing

When Maximilian enters the staff kitchen not much later, Sabrina is about to fix herself a cup of coffee.

'How are things?' Maximilian asks.

'Fine, thanks', Sabrina replies. 'I have handed in my essay this morning.'

'Cool', he comments. 'Then you'll have some time to catch your breath.'

'Yes', she says. 'He said he was going to read it this afternoon, though. Anyway, he has already left for the weekend by now. Maybe something's come up.'

She shrugs.

'He seemed unwell', Maximilian remarks. 'As if something had upset him. During lunch he was as always. Perhaps he has meanwhile been refused a replacement for Mrs Lohr.'

'Rahul was with him in his office', Sabrina states. 'I saw him leave, when I returned from my lunch break. He was not himself, either. I said hello, but he looked through me as if I weren´t there. Creepy.'

She shudders in recollection.

'Perhaps, something bad happened', Maximilian wonders. 'Bad news from his family perhaps.'

'Maybe', Sabrina replies. 'Let´s hope it´s not too bad. But when Rahul loses his composure … . I don´t think he is still here. And I´ll go home, as well.'

She puts her coffee cup into the dish washer and, while she is at it, the dirty plates and cups left on the work surface, as well.

'I´ll finish analysing this data set', Maximilian states. 'Otherwise, I´ll have to start again on Monday morning. Have a nice weekend.'

'See you on Monday', Sabrina says.

Maximilian is already at the door. He turns around once more lifting his coffee cup in greeting and walks along the corridor to his office. Meanwhile, Sabrina wipes the work surfaces clean before she, too, leaves the kitchen. Ambling along the corridor she notices that the door of Rahul and Alastair´s office is ajar. Alastair must still be there. She knocks at the door softly, then pushes it open cautiously. He is sitting at his desk with his head lying on his arms, asleep. Sabrina calls him by his name. When he doesn´t hear, she raises her voice, puts her hand on his shoulder and shakes it gently.

On waking up, Alastair is in a daze.

'I must have fallen asleep', he mutters pulling his shoulders up and leaning his head in turns to the right and the left.

'What time is it?' he asks finally, fumbling for his mobile under the documents in front of him.

'A quarter to three. — What about a cup of coffee?' Sabrina suggests. 'Not here in the kitchen, but in town. Or rather a glass of beer? What do you think?'

'Okay. Fine with me', Alastair replies. 'I am utterly useless today, anyway.'

'Off we go', Sabrina commands.

Outside the grey, chilly late autumn day enfolds them. Sabrina knows a bar, which he might like. A converted former corner tavern in the neighbouring quarter. A hidden gem, she says.

Alastair enjoys walking in the cold air. He feels wondrously refreshed. The fog in his head has gone. With a beer within easy reach life seems pleasant. For a while he just lives in the here and now. But then he remembers Teresa and a sense of guilt sneaks in. He should be on his way home. Yet, he feels too weak to change course. Resolving that he won't stay longer than twenty minutes, he continues following Sabrina along the narrow pavement. When he starts wondering where on earth they are heading, she turns around pointing in front of her.

'There it is', she says.

‚A pub', he remarks in amazement. The sign has caught his eye. On its emerald green grounding it features a young face with a crooked nose and prickly ginger hair, a blue captain's hat sitting on top. Under the image it says in Celtic calligraphy: *The Happy Skipper*.

'I like the sign', he says.

'Me too', Sabrina agrees. 'It was me who designed it, after all', she adds proudly. 'I live just around the corner, and as I passed by every day, I noticed that the bar was being redecorated. When I asked the craftspeople some questions, I met Sean O'Sullivan, the tenant. You'll like him. He is Irish.'

Sabrina opens the door and with her taking the lead they cross over to the counter where she says hello to the landlord, a tall young man in his mid-thirties, the image on the sign come alive. He is wearing a green and white flannel shirt with rolled-up sleeves. Both his face and his arms are covered by freckles. An emerald green apron imprinted with a downsized copy of the pub sign on its bib, almost reaches to his knees.

After exchanging a few remarks with Sean, Sabrina introduces Alastair to him.

'A fine pub', says Alastair, looking around. 'Good idea to use barrels for tables and to hang up the model yachts. I believe I can hear and smell the sea', he enthuses.

'I built them myself', Sean explains with a broad Irish accent. 'Scale modelling has been my hobby since my youth. My father was a crane operator at the freight port of Cork, and I have always been fascinated with seafaring. Then I got interested in historical yachts. It was always a big deal when one of them was moored at the quay. But I didn't become a sea captain. My parents were against it. They wanted me to study at university. Now, I run a pub called *The Happy Skipper*.'

He smiles rather wistfully.

Alastair resolves not to tell him about his grandfather who took him out yachting and taught him to steer a sailing boat when he was a youth.

'You've seen the sign, I suppose', Sean adds.

'Yeah', Alastair laughs. 'Nice work!

'Sabrina here, gave me some advice', replies Sean.

Sabrina and Alastair order a pint of Irish draught beer each. Sabrina insists on paying for them both and buys two small packets of crisps to go with them. While they are waiting for their beers, Alastair asks Sean how it came about that he ended up here. Sean tells him that after spending his year abroad studying at the local University, he wanted to set up shop in this town by all means. But he had to finish his master's degree at Cork, first. After graduation a compatriot offered him a job at a pub in Dortmund. He taught him how to run a business. When he came across the advert about the old tavern available for rent, his employer assisted him with the financing of the renovation.

As soon as Sean has put their glasses in front of them, they move on to a table at the window and sit down on the bar stools in front of it. When they have settled down, they lift their glasses saying 'Cheers' in unison.

'So what do you think?' asks Sabrina after their first sip.

'Delicious', says Alastair. 'And Sean has had an interesting life.'

Sabrina nods in agreement.

'Yes. I hope that word about *The Happy Skipper* is going to spread fast', she states. 'There is not much room inside, but in spring Sean can put up tables outside. It´s a long season, here, often starting with warm days in March or April and going on until mid-October.'

'This pub seems important to you', Alastair remarks.

'Oh, yes', Sabrina admits. 'As Sean has said I gave him a few tips. To use barrels as tables and bar stools, for example. There is already so much on offer that it´s vital to have something out of the ordinary, as a trademark so to speak.'

'Cool. Well done', praises Alastair. 'You have been beaming all over while talking about it.'

'Yes. This is what I really want to do', Sabrina enthuses. 'Design stuff for businesses. Space, logos, merchandise. This is what I am good at besides organizing and networking.'

'And what about your thesis?' Alastair asks taken aback.

Sabrina shrugs her shoulders:

'I would like to finish it. But afterwards I am going to make a new start', she says determinedly.

'Good luck', says Alastair, still amazed. He lifts his half-empty glass.

'Cheers. To your future', he says. They click glasses.

After a short pause Alastair asks:

'And how are you getting on with your thesis?'

'Quite well', Sabrina replies. 'I have handed in my essay today. Thanks again for your advice. And how are you?'

'I am unbelievably tired', Alastair complains. 'It's almost impossible for me to concentrate. You have seen it yourself. Sometimes I fall asleep sitting at my desk.'

'Of course, this is not easy at the moment', Sabrina says compassionately. 'I don't have any experience with babies, but when they get older, they'll certainly sleep better', she adds to comfort him.

'Let's hope so. As everyone affirms this, it must be true', says Alastair with a wry smile.

He lifts his glass to empty it and looks at his watch.

'I am sorry, but I have to go home now. Thanks for the beer', he adds getting up. 'See you on Monday.' He turns towards the door with a wave, avoiding to give her a hug, and rushes off. If he hurries – ten minutes to the tram stop in the town centre, fifteen minutes by tram and another ten-minute walk home – he'll be there in forty-five minutes and without arriving later than usual.

When he enters their flat, Fatima is sitting in the living room with Teresa.

Work and family

When it is quiet in the children´s room, Jakub, who has just finished emptying the dish-washer and making tea, enters the living room and takes his seat next to Ela on the couch. While sipping at his tea, he gazes at the enlarged and framed photo above the TV. It is their wedding photo with the bridal couple at the centre and the children, two-year-old Anna in her frilly white dress and four-year-old Leo in a dark suit and bowtie, in the foreground. His brother, who was his best man, is standing next to Ela, while her sister, her matron of honour, is at Jakub´s side. It is a beautiful photo. He has turned to Ela, and they are smiling at each other. The children, however, look at the camera with solemn faces, as if they were bearing the responsibility for their joint enterprise.

'You are so absent-minded today', Ela remarks. 'Any trouble at work?'

He tells her about Mrs Lohr and his worries concerning a suitable replacement for a longer time. Then he remembers Teresa.

'Aah. It has completely slipped from my mind again', he exclaims. 'Do you remember Teresa Rinaldi, the reserved but smart young woman on my staff who has a baby? Her partner is Alastair Collins, that brilliant young Englishman: stout, reddish-blonde, slightly darker three-day stubble. As I see it, she is as highly qualified as him, but almost too modest. The point is that she does not get much support. Neither her parents nor her in-laws live around here. During her farewell party I suggested that you could call her because of baby clothes we might still have. That was months ago.'

He shakes his head about his forgetfulness before adding.

'I have her phone number in my purse.'

Ela is shocked and amused at the same time.

'*You* offered that *I* would be ringing her up?' she exclaims.

'I am sorry', says Jakub regretfully. 'It was in the spur of the moment. I didn't have a better idea.'

Ela sighs:

'All right. The problem is that I gave away our baby clothes before we moved to Germany. But I could ask the Kims. If you believe that I can do her good with this. Or is there another reason?' she asks leaning sideways and gazing at him quizzically.

'No, of course not', replies Jakub. 'It is simply — my staff tell me that she seems to be about to over-stretch herself. Apparently, as with her work she strives to be perfect as a mother, too. Besides, she is worried about her future. Perhaps you could meet her at a café and have a chat.'

'Anything else?' Ela replies indignantly. 'You remember, don´t you, that I am struggling to balance work and family, too? By the way, there is little hope for change if she is so fixated on her chores.'

'Yes, you are right', Jakub admits. 'But still, it would be nice if you could get in touch. Anyway, I´ll do the shopping tomorrow and cook something for dinner.'

'That´s a deal', Ela says placably and puts her hand on his while their eyes meet briefly.

'The evening news?' he suggests and reaches for the remote control.

'Alright. It´s time', she agrees.

Their conversation has made him feel better although he did not tell her everything. Did she notice? Poor Rahul. He is suffering agonies. Jakub feels for him, and still, he does not want any unpleasantness. In return for peace, he´ll live with the sting of the sweet old pain which is love. Okay, it has always been more painful than sweet, but he is able to endure it because he has so much. Ela and the children are his home. It is fine by him the way it is. Of course, as a young man he was madly in love more than once. With Andrzej when he was a student in Gdansk, for example. They used to meet secretly sometimes. In public, however, they were just good friends. That was hard enough. But Tatuś, Mamusia – it would have broken their hearts. Perhaps she guessed that he was different. Now and then, she asked him about his love life. After all, a partner is a necessary ingredient to a good future, she said. His research grant at Yale

University was liberating. Everyone congratulated him to his success, and this made his parents accept the vast distance between them without a murmur. Then he obtained the professorship in Germany. Before moving to his new workplace, he married Ela. Meanwhile his parents have resigned themselves to the fact that he won´t have children of his own. That he visited them only twice a year was due to his demanding job. He can understand Rahul very well. He just couldn´t bear it any more. The pent-up emotions. He wonders how he is doing, now.

Chapter Four

October 2000

Speculations

Sabrina and Maximilian are standing in the kitchen deep in conversation, each cradling a cup of coffee. Now, Fatima walks in and after her Alastair. While the former fills the electric kettle, the latter pours himself a cup of coffee.

Sabrina turns to Alastair:

'Do you know anything about Rahul?'

'He wrote me an e-mail saying that he is ill', Alastair replies. 'A bad cold. It must have started on Friday evening.'

'Poor Rahul', says Fatima compassionately. 'I am a bit under the weather, too. Some virus going around, maybe.'

'Probably', Alastair agrees. 'Good for us if he stays at home as long as it is infectious. Teresa is terribly anxious about Georgie catching something.'

Sabrina ignores the change of subject:

'When I saw Rahul last on Friday afternoon', she insists, 'he was just leaving Professor Feldmann´s office, evidently all upset. I had never seen him like this before.'

'This is just your imagination running away with you as usual, Sabrina', Maximilian exclaims. 'So what´s the story you have thought out this time?'

'I don´t believe that Rahul likes women', Sabrina states shrewdly.

Alastair enquires suspiciously:

'What do you mean?'

'In any case, not the way you do', she explains looking at Alastair and Maximilian. 'Or can you imagine that he is going to fall in love with me or Fatima?'

In the wake of her remark there is much mumbling interrupted here and there by a laugh, which indicates that they are baffled and not a little amused.

Alastair shakes his head.

'You don´t have to fall in love with a colleague', he remarks not without self-irony. 'Besides', he adds darting a roguish glance at Fatima, 'it is your work that takes first place with you anyway, doesn´t it, Fatima?'

Fatima nods her assent.

'He is very nice', she says smiling, 'but I am glad that there is no spark.'

Sabrina is getting impatient.

'Of course, you know what I mean', she insists.

'Would you like us to infer that he is homosexual?' Alastair asks. 'Come on. He is just different because he is a Brahman. Didn´t you get that they have arranged marriages?'

'Do you suppose that his parents wrote him an e-mail on Friday afternoon saying that they selected a partner for him?' Sabrina mocks. 'After reading it he went to see his boss in his office and told him about it. In the end the news upset him so much that he fell ill. And Professor Feldmann was in shock, too. Something unsettled him so that he went home earlier than usual.'

'She is not entirely wrong', Maximilian mediates. 'The boss wasn't quite himself on Friday afternoon. But it doesn't make sense to go on speculating. After all, it's not our business. You'll see. Rahul will be his old self again when he is back on Wednesday. By the way, I have work to do', he says heading for the door.

They all follow his example except Fatima. She stays until the others have disappeared in their offices. Then she knocks at Alastair's door.

'Do you have a minute?' she asks.

'Yes, of course', Alastair replies looking at her questioningly.

'Have you told Teresa where you were on Friday afternoon?' Fatima enquires

'What do you mean?' Alastair retorts.

'I saw you leave the building with Sabrina', she explains.

'I was so knackered that I was unable to work', he explains irritably. 'We just went for a drink somewhere.'

'With Teresa tied down at home with Georgie?' asks Fatima indignantly

'Come on, Fatima. Just this once', he pleads to win her over. 'Besides you were with her, then. This really cheered her up', he says evasively and with renewed confidence.

'And?' Fatima insists. 'Did you tell her?'

Alastair looks through her haughtily and remains silent. After a while Fatima turns around wordlessly and walks along the corridor back to her office.

Tears

Alastair left work earlier than usual to help Teresa and to cook something delicious for dinner. When he enters the house, however, the pram is not in the hall behind the front door. So Teresa and Georgie are out shopping or gone for a stroll. The baby blanket with some of Georgie's toys on it is spread on the living room floor. His cot is in front of the window where his desk used to be. They have moved it to a corner in the bedroom, which is quite crammed as a result. Thus, they can just about manage, but soon they'll need at least one more room. With the high rents around here, it won't be easy to find a flat, not to speak of one which is both decent and affordable. Now he hears steps and the scratching sound of a key at the lock of the door. He opens it from inside and relieves Teresa of the carrycot.

'We were out for a walk', Teresa explains after their hello kiss. 'You are home early today', she remarks.

'Yes. I wanted to surprise you', he explains.

When asked about her day, she updates him:

'Georgie is able to turn from his back to his tummy, now', she reports proudly. 'He did it several times in the course of the morning. He skipped his midday nap, though. Could he already be teething? Only when we went outside an hour ago, did he fall asleep.'

'This probably means good-bye to sleeping to-night', Alastair remarks.

While locking eyes, each notices how drawn the other looks. They have sat down on the sofa, with Georgie between them in his carrycot. Now, Alastair gets up and lifts it asking Teresa to move closer to him. Then he puts it on her other side so that he can sit next to her. He puts his arm around her and says as he has often done recently:

'We'll get over this, you'll see. He is bound to sleep better, soon.'

'By the way', he remarks. 'Rahul was ill today. For the first time since we met. On Friday he already seemed beside himself, but I can't presume to be a reliable observer. I was so tired after lunch that I dozed off at my desk.'

She looks at him smiling.

'Oh, you didn't tell me about this on Friday.'

'It dropped my mind', he replies unable to look her in the eyes.

'Okay', he adds with an effort. 'I haven't told you all, but there is no need to worry, do you hear?' he pleads.

He recounts that Sabrina woke him up and led him to the pub she helped design. That the pub sign with the image of Sean, the Happy Skipper, was her work, too. And that she has a passion for interior decoration and plans to give up doing research after her doctoral degree.

'On the way there I wished I hadn't joined her', he says ruefully, 'but at least I was able to find out something interesting', he adds with a wry smile.

Teresa listened to his report with mixed feelings. On the one hand, she felt more at ease, now, because he was apparently driven by his familiar curiosity about other people. On the other hand, it has raised fears about Sabrina´s charms which had lain buried deep inside her. Still, Alastair´s sincerity encourages her to open up, as well and to talk about her nagging jealousy. Finally, she confesses to always wondering if he flirted with her.

'Do you remember the party we had after we were notified that our project would be extended?' she asks while the sadness she has held back for so long wells up. Tears roll down her cheeks.

'The hair on her sleeve', she manages to add between sobs. 'This is how you courted me, too.'

Without speaking, he takes her in his arms, and she snuggles up to him. The sorrows which have accumulated over months are finally being drained out. He kisses her cheeks again and again and while kissing away her tears, he senses the warm salty drops on his lips and tongue.

'I truly love you', he pledges, 'and I'll stand by you.'

Finally, he cups her cheek with the palm of his hand and asks:

'Is it because of this that you have been so scared of leaving Georgie alone with a babysitter, Resa?' he asks softly.

She loves this term of endearment which he alone uses. Without speaking she nods, still in tears. He passes her a tissue smiling at her.

'Nobody is going to call you a bad mother or me a bad father, if we look around for some support', he says. 'You have to take care, Resa. It's no use wearing yourself out.'

She nods again leaning her cheek into his hand.

In the silence they suddenly hear a rustling in the carrycot next to them, then a prolonged sound faintly reminiscent of an electric lawn mower. They both freeze and listen.

'Bwwwwwwwww, bwwwwwwwwwwwwww', they hear.

It is Georgie who produces this sound with his lips. They laugh, turn to him and watch their baby's doings happily.

Life partners

Jakub has just returned home from work. He hangs his jacket on the wardrobe, parks his briefcase in his study and goes through to the kitchen where Ela is busy chopping vegetables on a wooden board. On his greeting she turns round and looks at him.

'Hello Jakub. How was your day?' she asks.

'Not bad', Jakub says. 'Surprisingly, the replacement for Mrs Lohr can start on Wednesday. Do you remember Mrs Otto? I already had her as a stand-in some other time. She knows her way around and will settle in in no time. She is motivated and self-reliant.'

'This sounds good', Ela remarks.

'Definitely', Jakub confirms. 'However, she is much livelier than Mrs Lohr', he adds with a smile. 'Very sociable, in fact. She knows everyone in the department, and everyone knows her. When you have business in her office, she always gets you to chat with her.'

He laughs.

'And what about you?' he asks.

'At work nothing special, but I called Teresa and asked her what she needs', Ela recounts. 'We are going to meet in the *Café in the Meadows* on Wednesday afternoon at three thirty. Susanne Kim has given me quite a lot of children's clothes: some bodies, which always come in useful. Trousers, sweatshirts, tights and an anorak for the winter. Really beautiful things. Teresa will be overjoyed.'

'Thank you for making this effort', says Jakub. He is relieved.

'Now that I have fulfilled your wish, I would like to know what really happened at work on Friday', Ela demands.

'Could we postpone this till later when the children are in bed?' Jakub pleads. 'Please', he adds miserably.

'Is it so serious?' Ela asks with a quizzical look. Their eyes meet. He looks tired all of a sudden and also very sad.

'No problem', she says reassuringly.

After the usual bedtime ritual in the children's rooms – actually one big room provisionally divided into two small ones – Ela retreats to the living room while Jakub makes tea for them in the kitchen. He is feeling extremely uneasy. The thought of really telling everything terrifies him. Finally, he puts the teapot, two cups, sugar and a bowl of biscuits on a tray and carries it into the living room. Ela is sitting on the sofa lengthwise and with her legs propped up on a cushion, her favourite posture. After putting his treasures on the sofa table, he sits down in his armchair and pours tea into each of their cups.

'Ginger and Orange', he says forcing a smile. It is her favourite tea. While they are taking their first sips neither of them speaks.

Sensing that it can't be delayed any longer, he finally sighs deeply:

'All right', he brings out. 'When I was in my office on Friday afternoon, Rahul Sabharwal from my research staff came to see me. He is the man with roots in India. Quiet, highly intelligent and motivated. I had a sense of foreboding when he closed the door. But apparently, he only came to remind me of my promise to support Teresa.'

'How kind of him', Ela interjects. 'It is so good of your staff not to let her down now that she has a baby.'

'Yes', Jakub replies. 'Some of them make a real effort to look after her. Fatima, for example.'

Jakub takes his cup from the table and cradles it between his hands. Looking at the fragrant amber liquid, he forces himself to breathe before he continues.

'All of a sudden, Rahul burst out saying that he loves me', he says almost inaudibly and without raising his eyes.

'And what about you?' Ela asks holding her breath. 'Are you in love with him?'

Jakub senses that she has tensed.

'I want everything to remain as it is', he says softly and adds overcome by emotion:

'Admittedly, I am fond of him, but you are my life! Besides, a relationship with one of my staff members is incompatible with my position', he adds stiffly. 'I have told him this.'

'Did you tell him that you love him, too?' Ela asks.

'No, but he does not doubt it. What is love?!' he bursts out. 'I might have a crush, but I don´t love him as I love you. Don´t worry. Everything will remain as it has been.'

'But isn´t it strange when you meet at work?' Ela asks.

'He was off sick today', Jakub replies looking at Ela meaningfully.

'The poor young man!' she exclaims.

'Haven´t we all gone through this or something like it?!' Jakub remarks. 'That we are not allowed to live out our love!'

He gets up, sits down on the edge of the sofa beside her and kisses her cheek.

But this is not the end of his troubles. He told Sabrina today that he hadn't read her essay, yet, that something had come up and that he needed some more time. In fact, he wants to have a closer look at it. He is quite certain that he has already read some of her passages somewhere else, literally, maybe even in a paper from his own team. Tomorrow, he won't have time, though. A series of meetings. He sighs.

Temptation

On the next day Rahul is back at work. He still seems under the weather, but tries hard not to let it show. After the lunch break Sabrina leaves her door open on purpose. She waits till Alastair has gone home. Then she knocks at Rahul's half-open door and asks him to help her with a computer problem. He complies willingly and walks after her to her office where he shows her what to do in order to solve it.

While he is waiting till he is sure she can manage on her own, she asks him if he'd like to have a cup of coffee in the staff kitchen with her. So far they have talked shop, but now that they are leaning against the work surface with their cups in their hands, they have run out of things to say, and an awkward silence falls. This is a good opportunity for Sabrina, to bring the conversation round to personal matters.

'How are you?' she asks.

'Not quite well, yet', Rahul replies.

'Why didn´t you stay at home another day to recover properly?' she enquires.

Rahul does not reply.

After a pause Sabrina remarks:

'By the way, I saw you leave Professor Feldmann´s office on Friday. You were beside yourself. Was anything the matter? You looked through me.'

'It was nothing', Rahul says. 'Just a difference of opinion.'

'You do like the boss, don´t you?' she ventures. 'And he turned you down.'

'This is not your business, Sabrina', he says forbiddingly.

He gets up and makes for the door.

'Is he really gay?' Sabrina asks curiously.

Rahul leaves the room not deigning to answer her question.

A silver lining

When Ela opens the door of the *Café in the Meadows* it is already some minutes past three thirty. She looks around. There is a woman with a pram next to her at the window in the corner. This must be Teresa. The baby is sitting on her lap playing with a coffee spoon.

It gazes at Ela with big, questioning eyes while she introduces herself and sits down opposite them.

'I am Ela Feldmann, Professor Feldmann´s wife', she says. 'Hello Mrs Rinaldi. Hello Georgie.'

She smiles at him. Then she turns to Teresa.

'Nice to meet you', she says warmly. 'He is already quite a big boy. Nothing escapes his eyes.'

She smiles.

'I was afraid of missing you', Teresa explains. 'So I came earlier and ordered some tea.'

'Before I forget', says Ela. 'I have found some baby clothes. For the next few months.'

She passes her the big carrier bag. Teresa peeps inside and exclaims happily:

'How beautiful! Thank you so much. And even a pair of shoes. This is so kind of you!'

'And how are you?' Ela asks.

'Georgie is cutting his first teeth', Teresa recounts looking at Georgie tenderly. 'During the day he lets himself be diverted with toys, or he watches me while I do household chores with his teething ring in his hand shaking and chewing it in turn. When we go for a walk, he is content, too. But he wakes up several times during the night. When one of us carries him on their arm, he calms down right away, but as soon as we lay him down again, he whines and cries. We take turns. Still, we are quite worn out by now.'

'This sounds exhausting. I'll never forget what it was like with my children. But it'll get better sometime soon. — Probably, this is something you hear quite often', she adds smiling.

'Yes. My parents have also told me this', Teresa agrees.

'You are from Italy, aren't you?' enquires Ela.

'Not really', Teresa explains. 'My parents moved to Germany before I was born. My father came as a so-called guest worker. But my grandparents and some aunts and uncles of mine live in Naples.'

'And your husband?' asks Ela.

'He is English. His parents live in Richmond near London. But we are not married, yet', she says sheepishly.

'Too bad, when one's parents live so far away', Ela remarks. 'When they can help out from time to time, both sides benefit. — So you are alone with your baby during most days?'

'Yes', Teresa confirms. 'It is not easy. Meanwhile I got to know a few mothers in our quarter. We meet once a week. But in the beginning I sometimes felt terribly lonely. I was used to working every day, mainly headwork. Analysing data, writing essays, preparing a seminar. Now I don't have the time for anything relating to my project. My brain doesn't work as well as it used to, either. I just can't concentrate. Therefore, I am afraid of not being able to do research any more after my parental leave.'

'This might be due to hormonal changes and compounded by your lack of sleep', Ela explains. 'Don't worry, it'll sort itself out.'

And after a pause:

'Would you like to talk about your career prospects?'

Teresa looks at her questioningly.

'I mean, would you like to return to work, soon, when Georgie is one year old, for example?' Ela enquires.

'I don't know', says Teresa anxiously. 'On the one hand yes, I do. Then I could keep my post at the university. On the other hand: isn't this much too early?'

'Perhaps there is a possibility to organize childcare for Georgie', Ela says cautiously. 'I know a nice woman with a Polish-German background who works as a childminder.'

She tells Teresa a little about her and promises to be present at their first encounter. Teresa is going to think about it and to take counsel with Alastair. She notes down the telephone number and e-mail address of Ela's friend.

'If you need someone to talk to, you are welcome to call me', Ela concludes and passes her her business card on which she had written her private number with a pen. 'I work with a psychological support centre for families', she explains.

When they finally say their good-byes in front of the café, Teresa feels unburdened and optimistic. She resolves to visit her colleagues at work before going home. A look at her mobile phone, however, tells her that it is already half past four. Hopefully, Alastair will still be there.

Feedback

At two p.m. on Friday afternoon Jakub has an appointment with Sabrina to give her feedback on her essay. In order to be able to collect himself in advance, he takes care to keep his lunch break short. He is not hungry, anyway and only eats a salad.

At two o´clock sharp there is the expected knock at his door. He offers Sabrina a seat at the coffee table he uses for small meetings and starts by asking her how she is and how she is getting on as a member of his team. Then, breathing a sigh, he turns to Sabrina´s essay.

'Your thesis, the table of contents and the structure are promising', he elaborates. 'But some of the central passages are in fact quotes from other works.'

He opens the cardboard folder and puts it in front of her showing her the paragraphs he marked.

'It struck me because one of them originates from an essay of Maximilian´s I´ve read recently'.

'I wasn´t aware of this', says Sabrina, evidently shocked.

Jakub explains incredulously:

'In your previous papers and above all your master thesis you had to cite your sources properly. But it is not just this. A good essay does not consist of a sequence of quotes. Instead, your sources are the point of departure for your own line of reasoning.'

Sabrina lowers her head while Jakub continues with disapproval in his voice:

'I still assume that you know the requirements. Why didn`t you keep to them?'

'I didn´t have the time', Sabrina states in a low voice. 'I read and made excerpts, but I couldn´t develop my line of reasoning properly, any more.'

'All right', Jakub concedes. 'I am willing to regard this as a first draft, but I also had a look at your master thesis and found suspicious passages there, as well. I am going to have it checked by your former university.'

'No, please, don´t do this', Sabrina pleads.

'So you admit that you plagiarised?' Jakub probes.

'No. I did not do it', Sabrina says defensively.

Jakub looks at the folder in his hands shaking his head. Then he says firmly:

'You´ll have three more weeks for your essay. Is this enough? But I reserve the right to have your master thesis checked. After all, you don´t have anything to fear if you are innocent', he says reassuringly.

'Thank you', says Sabrina humbly.

'So that´s settled', Jakub confirms curtly.

He rises and opens the door for her. It makes him mad when someone just copies from other people's work and poses as the author.

Chapter Five

November 2000 - May 2001

The writing on the wall

When Jakub arrives in front of his office on Friday morning, the graffiti on his door catches his eye.

It features a chalk drawing of a penis and beside it in large letters the words *He is Gay!* with a smiley in place of the a. Panicking, he reaches for a tissue in his coat pocket and wipes over the area, but only manages to spread the chalk. The writing, however, is still legible. Hands shaking he unlocks his door and leans his briefcase on one front leg of the table. Then he races to the toilet, tears off some paper, lets water drop onto it and opens the door to the corridor. It´s too late. Mrs Otto, who stands in for Mrs Lohr, has heard him running past. When he hurries back, she is standing in the door frame of her office asking worriedly:

'What´s the matter, Professor Feldmann? Is anything wrong?'

As he passes by her without a reply, she follows him unbidden and just notices the word *Gay* on his door before he is able to delete it.

'How terrible! What an impudence! At our department of all places!' she calls out indignantly with her Bavarian accent standing out. And eager to help she offers:

'I´ll fetch a proper rag.'

She waddles off to the kitchen and reappears shortly after in front of Jakub´s office.

After wiping the door vigorously first with a wet, then with a dry cloth till it gleams, she pauses and exclaims regretfully:

'Ah, Professor Feldmann, we have made a mistake. We should at least have taken a photo as evidence for the directorate, or even the police.'

Jakub does not comment on her remark. Instead, while stepping out on the corridor once more to appreciate the result of her efforts, he says, outwardly calm:

'Thank you for cleaning this up, Mrs Otto.'

She is still upset. Meanwhile, Maximilian has arrived. When he opens the door to his office, Mrs Otto turns to him.

'Imagine, there was some scribble on Professor Feldmann´s door. Saying something about being gay. The impudence! I am off to check with the others if they have anything like this, too. The impudence … ', she mumbles.

'Please, Mrs Otto, calm down and don´t go', Jakub objects, but she doesn´t listen. She´ll just spread the news all over the place, he thinks, horrified.

'Are you all right, Professor Feldmann?' Maximilian asks.

Jakub jumps, when he notices Maximilian suddenly standing beside him.

'Of course not', he snaps.

'But thanks for asking', he adds placably.

'Do you have any idea who might have done this?' Maximilian inquires.

'No', says Jakub spontaneously. 'Let's forget about it. It said *He is gay.* Nothing insulting, after all.'

He does not mention the sketch of the penis.

'And if it happens again?' Maximilian insists.

Jakub makes clear that he does not want to pursue the matter any further.

'Someone has played a hoax on me', he placates. 'It's probably a once-off. Perhaps I was even a random target. Let's start doing our jobs. I have to prepare for a meeting.'

After arranging to meet for lunch at half past twelve, they withdraw into their respective offices. Jakub resists an impulse to close the door behind him. He wants everything to be the way it has always been, especially with Mrs Otto about to return any minute from her scouting expedition. Indeed, she reappears soon after in order to report that he was the only one with such a scribble on his door. Now, everyone knows, he thinks. The writing on the wall.

Exit

Returning from his lunch break in the university canteen, Jakub enters his office. So far he has coped quite well, although it took an enormous effort to smooth over his colleagues' well-meant enquiries. Even the university rector asked him for a word. He was being very sympathetic and offered to initiate an investigation. Jakub spoke out for letting the matter rest as long as it did not occur again. The fact that the evidence had been destroyed finally convinced his superior.

Now, someone is knocking on his door. He is expecting Sabrina who handed in the new version of her essay a few days ago, and she is on time. Under her trademark black blazer she is wearing a T-shirt with the image of a man's head on it. His short ginger hair stands up all around his face like a hedgehog's pricks, and he is wearing a blue captain's hat. The caption in an ancient script reads: *The Happy Skipper*.

Jakub rises and asks her to take a seat at the conference table in the corner. After some kind remarks to break the ice, he says:

'I am glad that you have been able to turn the corner, as the saying goes.'

She smiles and looks at him expectantly.

'This is the level I require from my doctoral candidates', he explains. 'Very promising, indeed.'

'Thank you', she says, still smiling. 'I am glad that you like my paper, but in fact, I don't want to go on.'

Has he misheard? Not go on? What on earth does she mean?

'You can't mean your doctoral thesis, can you?' he enquires.

She points at the front of her T-shirt and says:

'I designed these T-shirts, and I really enjoyed it. They are merchandise for the pub *The Happy Skipper*. I also helped with the interior design. This is where my talent lies.'

Jakub is left speechless. He struggles for words.

'What a pity', he says finally. 'I am sorry to lose you.'

He looks at her searchingly.

'Thank you for your kind words', she replies.

After informing her about the necessary formalities, he rises to say farewell. While they shake hands, she locks eyes with him and says out of the blue:

'It wasn´t me.'

As he remains silent seemingly confused, she adds:

'The scribble on your door. I didn´t do this. I don´t do such things.'

'Good of you to tell me', he mumbles. Resolved not to follow this up, he opens the door for her.

While he closes it again, he senses his leg muscles getting soft, and he lets himself fall into his chair at the conference table. He smiles. An unexpected change for the better, he thinks.

During the day his thoughts circled time and again around this outrageous incident. Oh yes, he has been wondering who from his chair or from the department might have been the perpetrator, and Sabrina was indeed one of the prime suspects. It sometimes seemed to him that she watched him, and besides, he threatened to have her master thesis re-examined. Quite a strong motive. He did not follow this through, though. It must have slipped his mind. His stressful life. Or did he postpone it subconsciously? Due to his eternal kindness. Now the matter has resolved itself.

Sabrina would start a new life. If it was her, there would at least not be any new attacks on him.

Before setting out for home, he accesses his e-mail account. As yet, he hasn't had any opportunity to do so today. Now, he only answers the most urgent ones. This particular message, for example, which was forwarded by Mrs Otto. Someone from the students' newspaper is asking him for an interview. They do a series of portraits of the professors. He has heard about this. It is supposed to be popular. He can see that it might be of value to the students, might even boost their motivation. He suggests Monday at half past eleven. Forty-five minutes, an hour at the most, he thinks. He'll ask about his career and his research. This shouldn't be a problem. No need for any special preparation.

When, finally, he shuts down his computer he is surprised how fit he still is after all that has happened today. Only as he is sitting on the tram, is he overcome by exhaustion. It is like a tight win at football after a long struggle. Has he really won? He leans back and closes his eyes. When he gets off, the cold air of the November afternoon envelops him. It's a chilly embrace. The fog is so dense that the houses on the next corner are only towering dark shadows. The light is as dim as if it were already dusk. He shivers.

The interview

Jakub is sitting in his office. It is already eleven thirty-five, but the journalist from the student newspaper has not arrived, yet. If he goes on reading his mail, now, he is sure to be interrupted. How annoying. He hates people not being on time. Lack of respect. But with the knock on the door his anger evaporates. He turns round on his swivel chair, rises and welcomes the young man who looks down on him through horn-rimmed spectacles with a leopard spot design.

His name is Joachim Federkiel, and he studies German literature and political science. One day he would like to work for a prestigious national newspaper. For Jakub it is interesting to get to know a student from a different faculty. He is upbeat about the interview, now. It would be a chance to talk about the research going on at his chair.

But Federkiel is more interested in personal information. Later on, there would be another series about the research projects.

'Then, you have caught me on the wrong foot', Jakub says. 'But fire away.'

Of course, he is going to keep his promise. Nor does he object to the interview being recorded. However, he asks for a copy of the article in order to be able to review it before publication. Federkiel reassures him that this is the usual procedure.

The first subject is Jakub`s career. This is easy: He attended secondary school in a small town in southwestern Poland. Luckily, he is able to oblige the interviewer with some entertaining anecdotes from that time. After his military service he went on to study at the University of Gdansk.

'Gdansk', ruminates Federkiel. 'How interesting! Weren't there these strikes by the shipyard workers at the beginning of the 1980s. The campaign led by this union. *Solidarity*, isn't it?'

'*Solidarność* in Polish', Jakub prompts.

'Exciting, indeed!' Federkiel continues enthusiastically. 'Were you politically active, too?'

'Like many other students I took part in the strikes', relates Jakub. 'I admired the courage of the workers and was in favour of the reforms they demanded: better working conditions, reliable food supplies and more rights such as access to the media and a limitation of censorship. Due to the existing power relations, however, a transformation to a democracy with the rule of law and full-scale civil liberties was a big, far-away ideal.'

'Were you engaged in any organising of the campaign yourself?' enquires Federkiel.

'No', Jakub admits. 'I wasn't one of the leaders. I don't have it in myself to be an activist.'

'But isn't it a moral duty to do all one can to bring about a change for the better', Federkiel inquires.

'In retrospect it is easy to pass censure', Jakub replies. 'When you are in the thick of things it's more complicated. In the course of events I sensed that people can have enormous power when they organize themselves and cooperate. For instance, in 1980 Solidarność was officially recognized, which was one enormous step forward. But in a dictatorship resistance is dangerous, and why shouldn't the Soviet Union intervene with their tanks as they had done in Czekoslovakia in 1968 and in Hungary in 1956? In the end it was the Polish government who declared martial law. Many people were detained, others lost their lives in obscure circumstances. A large number of scientists, artists and other intellectuals left the country.'

'And what about you?' asks Federkiel

'As I was not one of the leaders, I felt relatively safe', Jakub elaborates. 'After all they could not hold everyone captive. So I decided to stay and to finish my doctoral thesis. It suits me to work underground, so to speak, similarly to a mole.'

He smiles.

'Do you imply that you spied for the government?' Federkiel exclaims scandalised.

'No, of course not', Jakub replies alarmed. 'I am referring to the work of a researcher, which remains hidden from the eyes of the general public if it is not immediately relevant. And still, if you do a good job and are lucky and keep digging, you might one day come across a nugget of knowledge, which can improve people's lives, when it's understood thoroughly and applied wisely, no matter if it springs from the humanities or the natural sciences.'

'You wanted to dedicate your life to the truth, but in a wrong world', says Federkiel critically. 'The philosopher Theodor Adorno states that this is impossible.'

Jakub struggles for a suitable reply. As yet, he has never seen it that way. However, if you have never lived in a dictatorship, it is easy to be an idealist.

But Federkiel has already switched off his recording device and continues speaking in the same reproachful tone of voice:

'If the truth is so important to you, why are you living a lie, if you don't have to.'

Jakub turns white with shock and his upper body is breaking out in a cold sweat.

'Why do you hide being gay?' Federkiel specifies.

'Where does this rumour suddenly come from?' asks Jakub, who has rallied a bit, in return.

'I have a reliable source', says Federkiel with a superior smile on his face.

'Can such a scribble on an office door be a reliable source?' he questions. 'It is slanderous. That's all it is', he adds in despair.

'My source is a witness', Federkiel replies. 'Of course, I pledged not to give away their identity.'

'I won't give you permission to publish this', Jakub stipulates struggling to keep his voice steady.

'This wouldn't prevent the rumour from spreading. It has already become common knowledge far beyond your department', Federkiel replies. 'You won't be able to suppress it, any more. You'd better take the bull by the horns.'

'What do you want me to do? Make public my private life?' Jakub asks indignantly.

He is aware that further denial doesn't make sense. The situation would only become worse. Telling the truth is better than the rumour running rampant. He must talk now, for Ela and the children's sake. To secure their survival. How much does he have to give away? He can still refuse his consent for publication.

Thus, Jakub tells Federkiel about his childhood shaped by the Catholic faith of his family and about his time at school in communist Poland. How he fell in love with a boy for the first time. The agonies he went through because he thought that it was *his* fault, that something was *wrong* with him. Even when he was at university, he was extremely cautious. Only in a small circle of initiates did he open up. For a while he met someone secretly in a deserted place outside of town, but in the long run he could not bear leading a double life. Meanwhile his mother began to urge him to go out with a girl. Later she would remind him in an anxious voice that it was finally time to get married.

'So you married your wife and had children with her for your mother's sake?' Federkiel asks incredulously.

Jakub pauses in order to find the appropriate words. The silence is interrupted by a knock at the door.

'Yes', he calls making an effort to raise his voice. It is a colleague, Professor Dr Eisenschmid. They had arranged to have lunch together.

'Are you all right?' Eisenschmid asks. 'It is so unusual that your door is closed at this time of day', he quips.

Jakub looks at his watch. It´s already twelve thirty.

'I am being interviewed by Mr Federkiel, a reporter with the student newspaper', Jakub explains.

'For your professor´s portrait?' Eisenschmid asks. 'I can´t wait to read it. Mine has already been published. Have you seen it?'

Jakub shakes his head.

'It´s a good idea, this series', Eisenschmid states and after a pause:

'All right, then. Let´s have lunch another time, soon.'

He withdraws his head and closes the door.

Jakub apologizes for the interruption.

'Where were we?' he asks. 'Oh, yes.'

He elaborates on his long friendship with Ela, on Ela´s failed marriage and divorce. He, Jakub, was not the children´s biological father.

It is not true that I married Ela out of pity', he explains. 'We met as early as December 1981 during a sit-in strike. It did not take long for her to see through me. Perhaps it was because of this that we got along so well. By now, we´ve come to love each other.'

When the political system changed around 1990, he seized the opportunity of his life: a research scholarship at Yale University. After five years in the US he obtained the vacant chair here at the department. As Ela was very unhappy in Poland after her difficult divorce, he married her to be able to take her and the children with him. They both hoped for a new and better life together in Germany.

'If all this is really published, it will put our family under a terrible strain. It would tear me apart if I had to leave Ela. How could Leo and Anna understand this?'

'There'll always be serpents' tongues', Federkiel remarks. 'But you'll win the hearts of many people, if they read your story from your own point of view.'

'I don't like being in the limelight', Jakub objects. 'The worst case would be if Anna and Leo suffered from this at school or at their sports club. You know what children can be like. And the adults, as well, of course. — When is the article due for publication?' he asks.

'In the December issue', says Federkiel. 'The publishing date is December 15. The deadline is Friday next week.'

'In time for Christmas', Jakub remarks sarcastically and emphasises once more that the content must remain a secret until he has given his permission for publication.

After Jakub has closed the office door behind Federkiel, he sits down at his desk. He is truly exhausted. The only thing he is able to do now is shut down his computer. Meanwhile it is half past one, still early, but he'll go home anyway. As soon as Mrs Otto is back from her lunch break, he'll clock out with her. She'll be fussing about him, speculating what kind of virus he might have caught. It'll pass, but in fact, for the first time in years he starts to feel really ill.

The skeleton in the cupboard

When he enters the flat, he forces himself to call out 'Hello, is anybody at home?' as cheerfully as usual, but no-one replies. Avoiding the bitter-sweet ritual, usually dear to him, of facing his mirror image, he goes on to hang up his coat immediately. In the hall he sees a message on the notice board written by Ela. They are in town buying new shoes for the children. Fine with him. Thus, he has gained some more time. He must look terrible. His legs are tired. His lower back is aching and his head is under pressure. He'd better rest for a while.

After putting off his shoes he goes straight to the bedroom, hangs up his jacket on the back of a chair and lies down in his shirt and trousers on his side of the bed, the one next to the door.

How pleasant to be able to stretch himself out. As always, the strain he was under has affected his muscles, too. He closes his eyes. Extracts from the interview start to play in his mind like scenes from a film: what he said about his friendship with Ela, their decision to marry, his time as a student in Gdansk and –

he groans with the memory of mental agony – Andrzej. Of course, he didn't elaborate on their meetings and the drama of their relationship more than absolutely necessary.

Then, he was afraid the others would notice their being more than just friends. Among his fellow students there isn't even one inseparable all-male couple. Not even one whose close friendship reaches back to their time at school or even their childhood and could thus be justified. They always go out in groups, the men to a pub after their football training or with their women partners to the cinema at the weekend. Thus, he and Andrzej end up meeting secretly at a solitary spot on the banks of the river Motlava. It takes him half an hour to get there on his old bike. While riding along the bumpy cart track, his arm muscles contract to absorb the shocks. Over there behind the hazel bushes not far ahead the narrow path to the river turns off. Applying the brakes he lets his bike roll cautiously, then pushes it a few steps downriver and seats himself on the summer meadow on the bank. Here, he is hidden from view by the dense brushwork behind his back. On the opposite bank the foliage of shrubs and trees likewise towers up forming a living green shield. The sunrays bring the colours to life and pleasantly warm the skin on his arms and legs. The sky is of a deep blue and entirely cloudless. He is looking forward so much to meeting Andrzej. They have abstained from seeing each other during the whole exam phase. While he is waiting his gaze wandering over the surface of the water, he suddenly sees an object looking like a block of wood floating towards him. It is a human body. Utterly horrified, he follows it with his eyes while it approaches with its back upturned.

Black curls, not quite shoulder length, are swirling around the head. A loose shirt in garish colours is puffed up like a stranded balloon. Andrzey's hallmark, the Hawaiian shirt. Oh, my God! It is Andrzej! He jumps up and slides down into the water, which is shallow along the bank. After a few steps, however, he sinks down to his hips. Realizing that he hardly makes any progress he calls out: Annndrzej!!! reaching out to him, but in vain. He is not close enough. Not yet. He struggles to move forward one step, then the next one, but Andrzej's body drifts by with the distance increasing irreversibly. In despair, he calls his name one last time. Then he lets his cold hands sink down. He is freezing. Now, it is him, Jakub, who is floating on the water with the sky above a dull monotonous white. No, it is not the sky, it is the ceiling of their bedroom. How long has he been sleeping? It is half past four. Outside it is already dusk. He had a dream about Andrzej. After so many years.

Soon after their last secret date he lost track of him. They had often quarrelled because Andrzej was jealous of Ela. He claimed that Jakub trusted her more than him. During his fits of passion he even accused him of being unfaithful while tears were running down his cheeks. He was unable to believe that a man and a woman could be friends without being romantically attracted to each other. Finally, Jakub could not bear it any more. They spent so much of their time together arguing. Trying to allay Andrzej's fears sapped his strength. Besides, he felt continually uncomfortable about his double life. When he finally told Andrzej that he did not want to go on like this, he took it surprisingly calmly, with dignity even. It was the end of their relationship. It didn't escape his notice that Andrzej dropped out of his university course and became a trainee in a factory. He wanted to work with his hands, he said, do something useful. Jakub still feels guilty. He can only hope that Andrzej's new start went well and that he is fine, now. Once more, the dream image of his body floating in the river flashes up in his mind. He pulls himself together and deletes it. No wonder that he is cold when he is lying there without a blanket. He swings his legs over the edge of the bed, gets up and pads towards the kitchen still feeling a little woozy.

Seeing him like this, Ela is worried. On her return she had opened the bedroom door and found him sleeping, something which had never happened before during their time together. While he is settling down at the kitchen table, she makes him a cup of tea. His voice is husky, now, and his limbs are aching. He has probably caught a cold.

He joins his family at the dinner table, but withdraws to the bedroom soon after. This time he undresses and puts on his pyjama before snuggling up in his blanket.

When Ela finally joins him, he wakes up and tells her all that happened. He has already deeply regretted that he had kept silent about the shocking incident on Friday morning. Ela cups his hand, which is lying on the bed cover, with hers. She feels shaken. Poor Jakub. How awful that it has come to this, now. Then fear for her children creeps in. Is there really no alternative to publishing the interview, or anyway his professor's portrait, with all that private information? They would have to find a way.

The confession

The next morning Jakub feels so weak that he calls in sick. He can hardly get his message across, so husky is his voice. This makes Mrs Otto so worried about him that she starts giving him advice about the most effective brand of throat lozenges. As she gets all worked up about it, he eventually interrupts her and hangs up.

He returns to bed on wobbly legs. From the bedroom he hears the children in the hall, the music of their voices, while they put on their shoes, jackets and school bags. Ela is sending them on their way with goodbyes and take cares, a happy world from which he already feels cast out. With his thoughts circling around a single subject, the interview and its consequences, he dozes off and drowses all the morning drifting in and out of sleep.

Suddenly he is roused by a familiar jingle. The telephone is ringing. It is Rahul Sabharwal.

'How are you?' he asks anxiously. And then:

'I must see you. It's urgent. May I come by in half an hour?'

Jakub's heart thumps. He would rather turn down the request, but he cannot. In half an hour. It'll be half past eleven by then. They would have more than enough time before Ela and the children return. What can be so pressing that Rahul wants to talk to him immediately? Since the recent incident he has been withdrawn and purposely formal although Jakub tried to re-establish their former friendly relationship. And now, he breaks through all the barriers and barges in on him at home where he is not protected by the norms of the workplace. He has only himself to blame. He could have declined except for the panicky undertone in Rahul's voice.

Jakub opens the wardrobe, takes out the dressing gown he has hardly ever used and wraps himself up in it. Then he enters the kitchen. Ela has left a thermos with camomile tea on the table for him. Gratefully, he pours himself a cup and fetches a paracetamol from the medicine cabinet in the bathroom.

Now, the doorbell rings. After opening the front door, he leads the way to the living room. While Rahul apologises profusely, underscoring once more the urgency of their meeting, Jakub points to an armchair in silence. He himself sits down on the sofa opposite.

'I can't really speak, but I'll listen', he croaks.

'I am so sorry', says Rahul. He is sitting upright on the edge of his chair. 'Do you remember that Friday afternoon? Believe me, I just wanted to remind you of your promise, but then I couldn't hold myself back any more.'

'I understand', nods Jakub.

'And still, it wasn't me', Rahul continues. 'I did not write this on your door.'

'What exactly?' Jakub enquires.

'The others said there was something about you being gay on your office door. It wasn't me. Please, believe me.'

This sounds credible to Jakub. Rahul neither seems to know the exact words nor that there was a drawing of a penis. So he refrains from digging deeper and instead signals to Rahul to go on.

,After our … ahem … conversation on Friday I lost all control of myself', Rahul reports. 'For a while I just wanted to be dead. I didn't want to see anyone. So I went all the long way to my shared flat on foot. Once there, I just put down my bag before setting out again to wander through the streets till my legs gave out. When I returned, I knocked into one of my flat mates, Joachim. He noticed that I was under the weather, and we talked for a while. I did not tell him anything at that point, though — about *us*', he added looking meaningfully at Jakub.

Jakub lowers his gaze.

'Joachim said he would be meeting friends in a bar and asked if I wanted to join them', Rahul continues. Beads of sweat have formed on his forehead, and his facial expression mirrors the agony of mind he went through. He wanted to drink himself unconscious, drain out all his emotions. He, who usually never drank, wished to be carried away with a current of forgetfulness.

Finally, he woke up in the arms of one of Joachim´s friends. The men laughed a lot while walking him home. They had to prop him up, almost carry him and ultimately to pull and drag him upstairs to his flat.

'No doubt they know that I am homosexual, but they are good men. They accept any sexual orientation. I am sure that Joachim´s friend is gay, too', he concludes.

As the general direction of Rahul´s narrative is evident, Jakub refrains from asking the all-important question. Indeed, Rahul now pre-empts it:

'It is most likely that I talked about you, as well. But hard as I´ve tried, I am unable to remember what exactly I said.'

'What is Joachim´s surname?' Jakub asks. The paracetamol must have taken effect. At least his brain seems to work better, now.

'Joachim Federkiel. He studies German literature and writes for the student newspaper.'

'So you were his source. I gave him an interview yesterday. Did you know about this?' he asks grimly, shaken by the humiliating memory.

'He said that it was for your portrait and that the focus was on your career as a professor and a researcher.'

'That's what I thought, too', Jakub remarks sarcastically.

'I am so sorry', says Rahul apologetically lowering his gaze.

'The scribble on my office door – anyone who overheard you in the bar could have done this', Jakub ruminates.

'Yes', Rahul admits, still looking down.

Jakub rises.

'Thank you so much for coming', he says. 'But I need to be alone, now and rest.'

He walks Rahul to the door and with relief closes it behind him. What he has told him makes sense. He was truly ashamed of his behaviour. Why did he confess? Perhaps he was afraid because he suddenly fell ill. Poor Rahul.

Animated by the new turn matters have taken, Jakub pads through the corridor to his study, boots up his computer and writes an e-mail to Joachim Federkiel. Quite certain that he'll be all right by then, he asks him to come and see him in his office at noon on Thursday. Then he tells Mrs Otto to somehow get her hands on the two most recent editions of the student newspaper and to send him the professors' portraits of his colleagues by fax. He also discovers an e-mail by Teresa in his mailbox. She informs him that having found a viable solution for the care of her child, she would like to take up her old post in May.

More good news, he thinks. He shuts down his computer and heads for the kitchen leaving the doors open to be able to hear the fax machine. For the first time since Friday he is really hungry. He puts bread and butter, ham and cheese and a boiled egg on the kitchen table with three leaves of lettuce to turn it into a healthy meal. Before he sits down, he switches the radio on and listens to the news programme they broadcast around noon while making sandwiches and tucking into them with delight. When he finally pours himself an espresso, the fax machine bleeps. He puts down his cup on the coffee table in the living room, fetches the two pages with the professors´ portraits and begins to read. He has met the colleagues at senate meetings. Nothing seems to have got in the way of their careers, nothing seems to have turned their lives upside down. Or they are particularly clever at hiding it. Nevertheless, he does not envy them. Without his experiences he wouldn´t be himself. But he has grasped now what a good catch he was for Joachim Federkiel.

Picking up the reins

It is Thursday. After returning from his lecture, he expects Joachim Federkiel, who indeed turns up at twelve sharp. A good sign, Jakub thinks grimly. He asks him to sit in the same chair at the conference table as on Friday. Federkiel reaches for his draft of Jakub`s professor´s portrait in his shoulder bag and passes it on to him. He begins to read.

'And what do you think?' Joachim Federkiel asks, after Jakub has finally put down the copies in front of himself.

'It reproduces almost literally what I told you on Friday', Jakub says. 'Although you switched off your recording device for the second part, my confession, so to speak. You have a good memory.'

'An invaluable tool for my job', Federkiel replies nonchalantly. 'And what have you decided?'

'As I see it', Jakub begins, 'there is no reason to publish the part about my sexual orientation and my family situation.'

Putting the two other professor´s portraits in front of him, he continues:

'I would like to have such an ordinary portrait, too. Of course, the anecdotes from my time at school and the part about the 80s in Poland may remain. With them you already have something special.'

Federkiel´s facial expression is all disappointment. 'Oh, please, don´t do this!' he protests. 'You are going to deprive me of the most interesting part of the story!'

'You did not get hold of this material in an honourable way', Jakub explains. 'Your source was a desperate, drunken staff member of mine, who did not have a clue what he was doing and who regrets it deeply, now. And I was under great pressure on Monday. I believed not to have a choice because of a possible vicious rumour. So you can't publish this with an easy conscience. You would violate the principles of good journalism before you even launched your career.'

Federkiel is not the one to give in so soon.

'I understand that you don't want to cause a great stir, but it is about something bigger than yourself alone', he argues. 'By coming out you could empower lesbians and gays, who still face discrimination in Germany, too. As popular as you are with the students of your faculty and beyond. Own up to your sexual orientation! Besides, how can you be so sure that the rumour has not spread? If so you'll have to come out, sooner or later.'

'I don't have to do anything, Mr. Federkiel', Jakub retorts. 'I insist that you cancel this part of the portrait. You have blindsided me, and now that I have been able to think again more coolly, I have come to the conclusion that I can't burden my family with a coming out, at least not now.'

'What a shame, but I accept your objection, of course', Federkiel says. 'I'll show you the final version of the portrait tomorrow. If you happen to change your mind, please get in touch any time.'

He reaches for the *Post It* block, which is lying in the middle of the table, and writes his name and telephone number on the note on top. Meanwhile, Jakub has already risen to open the door for him. He is glad that they have got to the end of their conversation. It has sapped his energy. Evidently, he has not completely recovered, yet. After the meeting he has to attend early this afternoon he´ll go home.

They had chewed over the question of his professor´s portrait again and again, when the children were in bed. Surprisingly, Ela´s initial concerns evaporated over time. She regained her composure and even seemed at peace with the world.

'We always reckoned that it would become public one day', she said with a smile. 'Why not now?'

'And Anna and Leo?' he asked taken aback.

'Why?' she enquired. 'They know that you are not their biological father, but they are aware what a good father you have been since you became a part of their lives. We belong together as a family and are going to weather out the storm together.'

As if to confirm this, she took his right hand between her two hands.

'Still, I am afraid that they would suffer from it', he objected. 'That their peers or even their parents would tease them, or call them names and insult them. If they were older, it would be another question.'

'We live in a liberal, pluralist and tolerant society, now', she replied.

How could she be so trusting of the world? he wondered. She, who had been faced with the carelessness and the prejudices, the malice and the baseness of her fellow human beings more than him.

Her optimism made her look younger than she was. She looked good although she must have had a long day, too. Where did she take the energy from? He felt an urge to yield and to let himself be led by her intuition. But after all he had gone through, he believed that he assessed the situation realistically and could not but choose what seemed to be the more convenient path hoping that thus, they would be left in peace.

A new beginning

Teresa is lying awake in her bed listening to Alastair's regular, calm breathing. Tomorrow is her first day at work, a Wednesday. So fortunately, she won't have to start with a full week. In retrospect, time has passed so quickly. On Sunday they celebrated Georgie's first birthday. They had coffee and cake with Fatima and Rahul and a mother from their child-parent-group, who had become a friend, with her one-year-old child.

Of course, she and Alastair are proud parents. They adore Georgie and admire every progress he makes. Yet, they have to be on their guard all the time, now that he is able to crawl about faster than you think pulling himself up straight not only at the sofa, but also at the book shelf and the kitchen drawers. They had to remove all the possibly dangerous things and keep them on a higher level.

In order to facilitate looking after him, they put up a playpen on his blanket in the living room. In there, he sometimes gets absorbed playing with his plastic cups. He puts a smaller into a larger one and then takes it out again. When he has had enough, he crawls to one side, pulls himself up and holding himself with one hand begins to drop his toys on the other side of the grid. Then stretching out his arm he points at an object and calls *Da, da!* in a plaintive voice with his face turned pleadingly towards her. This is his way of communicating that he needs her attention. As he sleeps little during the day, now, being alone with him all the time can be exhausting.

The last four weeks have been dedicated to settling Georgie in with their childminder. Agnes has two children herself, five-year-old Halina and three-year-old Jan. When they met, she wondered if this could really work: two small children and on top of this one-year-old Georgie? But meanwhile she has learned that she can trust Agnes. Jan is a little wild sometimes, but Halina is like an older sister to Georgie. By now, the family has almost become his second home. So much so that it hurts a little. This is the price she has to pay for the opportunity of being able to continue her career. And she knows that it was the right decision.

While planning to get back to work, her self-confidence increased so that she did not let herself be discouraged by her parents´ doubts. She felt strong, but the source of her strength did not lie in herself alone. Her thoughts wander to Ela, who encouraged her to take this step and who connected her with Agnes. She thinks of her boss Professor Jakub Feldmann, who has always let her know how much he appreciates her as a staff member and as a researcher and who has kept his promise to go on supporting her. And with a heart almost overflowing with love and happiness, she turns to Alastair, who has been a loving father and partner, who stands by her and her plans and has pledged to share the work with her.

It´s true that she had sometimes felt very lonely, but her fear that she would have to live in isolation, only herself and the baby with Alastair coming and going, was unfounded. Instead, a network has begun to develop around her little family. There is Fatima, her good friend, who after voicing some initial doubts has encouraged her plans throughout. She asked her to be Georgie´s godmother. Her colleague Rahul visits them regularly, and Georgie has quite taken to him. Alastair thinks that he would be a good godfather. Then, there is one of the mothers from her parent-child-group with whom she could exchange thoughts about their children and talk questions and problems through. And some weeks ago two girls from the neighbourhood asked her if she needed babysitters.

Now, they sometimes come by to play with Georgie, which gives her time to do some work.

One day they would invite all these people and everyone who has joined them by then, because she knows that networks grow once a beginning was made. They would have a big party. Their wedding, perhaps.